MR. DUDRON

A Public Space Books
PO Box B
New York, NY 10159

Printed in the United States
First edition, 2024

A Public Space gratefully acknowledges the support of the New York State Council on the Arts and the individuals, foundations, and corporations whose contributions have helped to make this book possible.

ISBN: 9781736370988
eISBN: 9798985976946

www.apublicspace.org

987654321

Also by Giorgio de Chirico

Geometry of Shadows

The Memoirs of Giorgio de Chirico

Hebdomeros

GIORGIO DE CHIRICO

MR. DUDRON

a novel

translated from the Italian by Stefania Heim

A PUBLIC SPACE BOOKS

NEW YORK

INTRODUCTION

Midway through *Mr. Dudron*, the titular character considers the way he is perceived by others. He is disappointed, he confesses, "when someone says I have the air of a sweet man, inoffensive and sentimental." Instead, he wishes people would see him as "a rabble-rouser" or a "bandit." He repeats this wish twice in the novel—like someone satisfied with an articulation they feel explains so much. But the tone of his stated desire is characteristically ambiguous. Does he mean it? Is he making fun of himself? Is he making fun of us? Though the book is full of Mr. Dudron's perceptions and memories, this is a distinct, even singular moment of self-reflection.

Giorgio de Chirico, for his part, spent decades considering Mr. Dudron. From the late 1920s through the 1970s, sometimes in French and sometimes in Italian, he wrote and published episodes tracking the frequently humorous misadventures of his hero—a painter who wanders, dreams, remembers, frets, polemicizes, and tells stories. De Chirico's first forays into imagining this character coincided with the 1929 French publication of his novel *Hebdomeros*—another hypnotic, largely plotless narrative following another semiautobiographical hero. As late as the 1970s, he was describing his "new" novel in interviews, talking about the work he had to do, promising to dedicate himself to it.

As with any text that remains unpublished in an artist's lifetime, we cannot know for certain if de Chirico ever settled definitively on *Dudron*'s final form. This translation is made from the Italian-language manuscript discovered by Paolo Picozza in the artist's archive, which concludes with de Chirico's customary "*Fin*" in a flourish by his hand. The Italian edition was first published in 1998, the twentieth anniversary of de Chirico's death, by the Giorgio and Isa de Chirico Foundation with Le Lettere in Florence.

In its long history of excerpting, revisioning, and reimagining, the novel you are holding underwent many permutations. "Monsieur Dusdron" in its first iterations, the maestro's name began as a reversal and collision of *nord* (north) and *sud* (south). It is also a collision of citations and suggestions: perhaps a reference to Pierre Reverdy's *Nord-Sud revue littéraire*, perhaps a riff on the allegorical significance of the cardinal points. As the name and textual history suggest, this book is multilingual, roving, playful, serious, fragmentary, shape-shifting.

The most curious of de Chirico's additions to the text is his incorporation in the 1950s of didactic musings on the history of art voiced by Isabella Far—she of the "philosophical spirit" and "exceptional intuition"—a character fashioned after the artist's second wife (the Russian Jewish Isabella Pakszwer who was, in real life, rechristened Isabella Far by de Chirico). As Dudron explains to her character in the novel, "your name has something oracular, something prophetic about it. In French it sounds like the word *phare*, the light that reveals the port to seafarers; in English, on the other hand, it means *far*, and indeed you do go very far with your thoughts, very far, but always with that overpowering logic that is the prerogative of superior spirits."

Several of the Isabella Far passages draw directly and quote extensively from a series of essays from the early 1940s collected in de Chirico's 1945 volume of critical prose, *Commedia dell'arte moderna* (The comedy of modern art). These pieces—"Form in Art and Nature," "Portraits," and "Still Lifes"—are read out loud in the novel by Mr. Dudron and a painter friend of his with "sound and normal ideas about art." In *Commedia dell'arte moderna*, the essays, which we know now were written by de Chirico, are also attributed to Far. Thus, just as a critical, theoretical mode muscles its way into his fiction, his essay collection was enveloped in a fiction of authorship, character building, and voice.

These are not the only earlier writings that are sutured into the body of this composite text. When, in a "tormented" mood, Mr. Dudron turns to his bookshelf seeking some guidance in his quest for painting's essence, he opens J. F. L. Mérimée's nineteenth-century tract *The Art of Painting in Oil and in Fresco: Being a History of the Various Processes and Materials Employed, from Its Discovery, by Hubert and John* [*sic*] *van Eyck, to the Present Time*. He proceeds to quote from both the preface and the book itself—a long passage about Jan van Eyck's use of varnish. In keeping with the polyvocality of the original, I have used W. B. Sarsfield Taylor's nineteenth-century translation of these passages in my own translation.

To some scholars, such passages—alongside other lengthy commentaries voiced by Isabella Far in conversations that punctuate Dudron's daily wandering and nightly dreaming—constitute the didactic heart of this text, de Chirico's fullest articulation of his theories of art. To others, they mar the narrative momentum, distract from the figurative and imagistic power found, for example, in stories of a snail-breeding industrialist or a monomaniacal artist obsessed with achieving the perfect mayonnaise that are allegories for the condition of art.

What strikes me is how surprisingly familiar de Chirico's hybrid, intertextual form feels in our contemporary literary moment. Genres like autofiction and autotheory play at the intersections of self and character, narrative and evidence, embodied experience, and ideas. I think of the dialogue about beauty, ugliness, genius, and art in Sheila Heti's *How Should a Person Be?* Or of María Gainza's digressive narration of a critic's life through the analysis of and stories about the work she encounters as she wanders around Buenos Aires in *Optic Nerve*.

With these works, *Mr. Dudron* shares an explosion of theory, creative practice, and messy, unmanicured bodily experience. The artist places all his garments upon his bed, layering on it also "an old ink-stained cloth" and "a few old newspapers that he found at the bottom of a drawer" to make it warmer, lies down to meditate on his painting in progress of "an ancient beach with a tranquil and solemn beauty," and then lets that painting carry him away. These texts and *Mr. Dudron* share complicated autobiographical characters engaged in self-questioning about the making of art when—as evidenced by the formal example of the texts at least—making art and living and theorizing are utterly entangled. They share bits of texts from elsewhere, scraps of evidence from their investigations and their journeys. Paolo Picozza calls *Mr. Dudron* "theory in the form of a novel." As with the recuperation of de Chirico's long-maligned late-career paintings through the lens of postmodern practices, perhaps these contemporary literary forms can help us approach the entirety of the shifting constellation of drafts, scenes, forms, and moods that make up *Mr. Dudron*.

For even beyond its textual history, this book contains so much. There are the generally hilarious, frequently moving descriptions of Mr. Dudron's adventures—as he shoves baguettes, pastries, "cans of sardines and tuna, slices of prosciutto and salami, olives, eggs, boiled potatoes" into his pockets and attempts to retain a dignified posture passing his wealthier neighbors, who can afford full pension at the hotel where they live, drinking "costly aperitifs" in the lobby. There is a beautiful ecopoetic passage tracing the journey of a hawthorn seed that follows a patient succession of mosses to lodge between the "blackened stones" of a bridge and finally become a robust plant hanging "in long garlands that moved unceasingly even in the gentlest breeze." There is a centaur family and there are three caged lions left alone in a suburban field while the manager of the fair goes to the police station for permits. There is the act of holding a pebble to the light to conjure "high noon in a rocky and wild place in the time of the Greek myths." There is a stunning description of the way air surrounds objects of different textures, allowing us to "see with our minds aspects of things that are invisible to us."

This very muchness exists in de Chirico's sentences themselves, which meander and wind and are full of complications and transformations. In a single sentence a few pages into the novel, a speeding car becomes first "an enormous flow of draining pasta water" and then a gigantic caterpillar as it lengthens and contracts and plunges dangerously between obstacles. As John Ashbery says of *Hebdomeros*, de Chirico's "long run-on sentences, stitched together with semicolons, allow a cinematic freedom of narration; the setting and the cast of characters frequently change in mid-clause."

Then, there is the temporal and spatial unfurling of those sentences. I wrote in my introduction to de Chirico's Italian poems, *Geometry of Shadows*, about the difficulty of retaining in English Italian's more elastic syntax—which he pushes to its limits. In this novel about an artist and a wanderer, it felt especially important to match as much as possible the order of de Chirico's clauses, as they lead the reader through space and among ideas, as though moving a viewer's eyes across a scene or a canvas. We follow in our imagination a "young, unmarried mother" as she crouches behind a church column, slowly realizing as a procession of people passes through the sentence that she is lurking at her baby's father's wedding. In a smaller but more typical example, I tried to refrain from making a descriptive detail antecedent to a noun as is customary in English and instead allow for the experience of the discovery of details de Chirico so frequently creates. Sometimes it feels like his sentences are literally carrying themselves away.

* * *

In a pair of late-career works, both called *The Return of Ulysses*, de Chirico paints a man in an undersized boat afloat in a small, unruly, cartoonish body of water somehow contained in the middle of a room. In the first, from 1968, a window opens out upon an arid, empty landscape with a single temple, and on the opposite wall hangs a variation of one of de Chirico's early metaphysical paintings. This man is young, dressed in white ancient garb, and rowing. In the 1973 companion, the man, now the color of stone as though midway through a transformation into statue, leans forward, reaching a hand toward the water. Two broken pieces of pillar float in the water beside him. This time the window is larger and looks onto a vaster body of water, with a promontory in the distance. Where the painting hung in the earlier work is now a doll-sized temple. The borders between fantasy and reality are more permeated here.

Through the wandering journey of translation, I kept returning to these paintings. Though many images in *Mr. Dudron* invoke de Chirico's visual art—his work is obsessively self-referential—I started to think of *The Return of Ulysses* as a visual encapsulation of the novel. The water sits where you might expect a bed; the rowing becomes an allegory for all the text's dreaming. The window, painting, and temple are visual echoes of the unceasing recollection of landscapes past—experienced, imagined, and painted—that make up so much of the actual terrain of the book.

I began to notice all the ways that *Dudron* functions as a retelling of *The Odyssey*. I recognized *The Odyssey* in *Dudron*'s divagations, the strangeness of its temporality, and, most of all, its almost formulaic return to the acts of narration and telling. Even the repetitive language marking Isabella Far's entrances and exits functions like epithets, grounding readers in the otherwise meandering story. I noticed among de Chirico's wending sentences many Homeric similes—elaborate comparisons yoking together different identities and modes of being, human machinations and the natural world—which are so central to the epic. De Chirico writes of Mr. Dudron: "Though he was laden with every kind of provision, he walked with his head high and his eyes straight ahead, as a wife in an advanced state of pregnancy walks, leaning on the arm of her legitimate consort on a nice Sunday afternoon." And in the humorous, allegorical scene of the mayonnaise: "Right at that moment some large night fliers burned themselves in the acetylene gas lamp and fell into the decomposed mayonnaise, writhing like wild ducks would in the water of a pond if shot by a hunter."

Mr. Dudron is Odysseus the storyteller (Dudron's sculptor friend is "enticed by the promise of hearing Mr. Dudron tell stories"). He is Odysseus returning home over and over and over again throughout the novel, having braved each day's ordinary perils. But he is also Odysseus trying to return home to some past, idealized state of art. For Dudron, as for Odysseus, that home is a kingdom threatened by antagonists—modern art critics falsely declaring their love just like Penelope's suitors. Each hero fears that home no longer exists.

Perhaps it is little sad, even a little pathetic, that Mr. Dudron—like de Chirico's painted Ulysses and like Hebdomeros, who also "went all around his room in a boat"—is trapped in the ordinary, nonheroic realm of a room or imagined fantasies. This is the strain of tender buffoonery, the gentle lampooning with which Mr. Dudron and myths in general are treated across this book. Aeolus and Boreas "puff out their cheeks like grotesque fountain masks and blow down on the earth and its people their never satisfied wrath" and Achilles and Ajax are two-liter bottles of wine dominating the other, smaller beverages on a table.

At the same time, though, the text demonstrates profound awe and respect for these prosaic things transformed by mythical imagination. For Mr. Dudron, a lizard on a sunny wall *is* "the dragon slayed by Saint George," not a reminder of the dragon or a humbler approximation. Humans live "below the immovable gazes and distant, smiling expressions of various Joves, Junos, and Hercules"—and it makes no difference to the immensity of that experience that these gods are statues. For, as de Chirico and Dudron both know, mysteries really *do* surround us, "like the sounds that furniture sometimes makes in the great silence of the late night." This book brings them to life.

—Stefania Heim

MR. DUDRON

It was a mild October afternoon, and Mr. Dudron, sunk deep in a folding chair, was having his siesta in his studio. As often happened when he was not working, his thoughts drifted to painting. "Painters these days," he said to himself, "—and really it has already been true for some time—painters do not create paintings; *they don't paint*; they just leave colors to dry on canvas. Now, a beautiful painting is never made of dry color, but of *beautiful colored material*. That is what Isabella Far told me one day in a museum in front of a painting by Velázquez. Isabella Far sees painting as few today see it. Her philosophical spirit and exceptional intuition enable her to thoroughly investigate the complex problems of painting that have gone forgotten for almost a century. I understand very well that she is misunderstood. It's been quite a spell (three-quarters of a century at least) since this precious Ariadne's thread has been lost. And perhaps it falls on me and on Isabella Far—the task of finding it again, and of offering it to painters, our contemporaries, who yawn so widely upon their palettes they dislocate their jaws, and who seek to preserve appearances with pretentious and skeptical attitudes that are ultimately nothing more than unhappiness and irritation.

After all, there are things to be unhappy and irritated about," continued Mr. Dudron to himself. "Painters working today no longer enjoy themselves. They all feel—in a very confused way, it is true—but they feel nevertheless that *this isn't working*, that *this won't work anymore*. Out of desperation some dive into the swamp of so-called invention or would-be spirituality; they seek to distract themselves and others by talking of inspiration, of lyricism, of wonder, of strangeness, of mystery, ah yes, *above all of mystery*. But all of these, alas, are nothing more than shortcuts, which, though they can at times, from a practical perspective, produce some results, are scarcely reassuring. And deep down, very deep down, everyone yearns with infinite nostalgia for that faraway land, that Lost Paradise of that fine, that *finest art*." At this point in his thoughts the formidable rumbling of an engine caused him to rise and approach the window. He saw stopping below, outside the door to his house, a magnificent automobile—long and lustrous like a terrestrial torpedo boat. A lady of his acquaintance emerged. She had blazing hair and was dressed with an elegance that was at once severe and sporty, which made of her something between Athena and a modern Valkyrie, but more Valkyrie than Athena. She entered Mr. Dudron's house like a gust of wind, and without either sitting down or wishing him good day, she began to speak rapidly and in a breathless voice, pacing back and forth across the room. "You must be ready, Maestro," she said to him, "by precisely seven this evening; I will pass by with the car to fetch you." Then she went on to explain, covering the studio with her great strides, that she had made a date with friends at an inn on a hill near a town located on the shore of a lake about fifty kilometers away. There, at that inn, an acquaintance of hers, a prosperous industrialist specializing in the manufacture of shotgun cartridge cases, had built a *snail farm*. "Apparently, Maestro," she said to Mr. Dudron, who was listening to her with a kindly and resigned air, "he has immense plots of land full of cabbages and lettuces of all kinds. He also has peach trees, many of them, because snails are gluttons for peaches. Across the fields, below the peach trees, in tens, in hundred thousands, in tens and hundreds of thousands, live the snails. When a peach that is overripe falls from the tree, the snails focus their eye-stalks on the fallen fruit like a squadron's guns on the fort of the enemy coast. Slowly but surely, they mount the assault; they cling like suction cups to the wretched peach, of which, in an instant, nothing remains but the pit, as dry as if it had been exposed for a week to the desert sun. Then, satiated, the voracious mollusks depart even more slowly than they came, leaving behind the trail that everyone recognizes. Before you eat snails you must purify them; to purify them, you starve them for a period ranging from five to eight days." These bold and colorful descriptions did not exactly encourage Mr. Dudron to eat those snails, all the more as he had a horror of mollusks in general and of snails in particular. He felt an innate aversion to anything flabby or lacking internal structure. This was one of the reasons he did not love the paintings of his contemporaries. But it would be a mistake to deduce from this that he loved hard materials; on the contrary, he felt no affection for materials like iron or steel. Even in painting he did not love hardness or rigidity; he did not love either the primitives or painters such as Mantegna and Botticelli. He made an exception for Dürer. "But Dürer *is not dure*," he was in the habit of saying, smiling beneath his mustache, "even if in his *Lives*, Vasari calls him "*il Duro*." For Mr. Dudron, the ideal material had to be tender and fluid but at the same time firm and solid. Therefore, his favorite painters were Veronese, Tintoretto, Velázquez, and Rubens. Mr. Dudron would have liked to recount all of this to the gentlewoman who was attempting to lure him toward the snail fields, but, whether because he feared that she would not understand a word and think he was suffering from a mental breakdown, or because his atavistic gallantry forbade him from contradicting his interlocutress, he pretended to agree, with enthusiasm, to the idea of going that evening to eat snails.

At seven precisely the same rumble he had heard in the afternoon alerted Mr. Dudron that the hour of departure had sounded. He went down and sat beside the modern Valkyrie. At once she took off at breakneck speed, but she drove with such confidence and mastery that the car seemed transformed: it was no longer an automobile constructed of metal and wood but something enormously elastic. It lengthened and contracted as necessary; it passed between two obstacles, grazing them with its metal flanks, emerging like an enormous flow of draining pasta water, with the movements of a gigantic, high-speed caterpillar, only to plunge between two other obstacles even closer together than the first. They were crossing the city's outskirts. At that hour numerous laborers, having finished work, were returning home on their bicycles. They were setting off toward their hearths, pedaling patiently and blocking the entire street.

They were pedaling patiently to their hearths where waiting for them were their wives, their children, their parents—everyone they loved, everyone to whom they were devoted above all else, notwithstanding the arguments that frequently erupted and the misunderstandings; even if, sometimes on Sundays, to relax and escape the tedium of family, to enjoy an hour or two of freedom, they abandoned their houses to go to the nearby tavern and meet their friends and coworkers. With them they emptied bottles of wine and cider and pitchers of beer, playing cards and billiards or, when it was nice out, bocce behind the tavern in the fenced-in courtyard, where the sunflowers peer.

Despite the fact that the street was crowded with vehicles of all types, the modern Valkyrie, with a confidence and ease that astonished and amazed Mr. Dudron, slid between one cyclist and another, metamorphosing her car into a kind of eel. She passed between a car and a pedestrian, between two pedestrians, with stupefying agility. Once they passed the city's suburbs, the car sped onto the wide roadway in the middle of the countryside. Meanwhile evening had fallen. To the north, toward those heights where they were heading, storm clouds had gathered. The wan lamplight made the black outline of the mountains leap out, particularly one mountain with a distinctive crenellated peak, which, practically bristling with enormous teeth, looked like the jaw of a felled dragon and had been dubbed the Great Saw. Finding herself on the empty road, the driver accelerated her pace. Mr. Dudron started to feel ill. With an uneasy eye he followed the speedometer: 65, 70, 75, 80, 105, 110, 115, 120, 125, 130.... One hundred thirty kilometers an hour and it was the dead of night; they were far from the city, and the storm was approaching rapidly from the heights where they were pointed. A few raindrops started to fall, making the road horribly slippery. Mr. Dudron was afraid. The darkness was complete; even inside the car, darkness reigned. Just one or two dials in front of the driver were illuminated faintly, with a bluish, cold, dull, lunar, unsettling light that made one think of clinics where deathly ill patients and those who have just been operated on doze off, or else of laboratories in future times, where strange and infernal inventions will be perfected by genius scientists with hydrocephalic heads, like those little monsters conserved under alcohol. Against the windows and sides of the car the incessant, biting wind rushed at ever-higher speeds. They crossed a village, half asleep. In the dim light at the foot of a park, Mr. Dudron glimpsed for a moment the monument that the townspeople had erected in memory of the monarch who in this area a few decades before had been struck dead by a regicide's dagger. This fleeting vision transported Mr. Dudron to the distant days of his own childhood. Like a scene at the theater that is illuminated gradually, the images took shape in his mind. He saw himself in his paternal house. Then, too, it had been a stormy night; his father had come home with a newspaper announcing in huge letters the assassination of the king. Mr. Dudron remembered his father's troubled and saddened face. On the walls of the study, among photographs of various locomotive models, hung two large portraits of the king and queen encased in frames of engraved black wood. Mr. Dudron's father sat at his worktable, on which there stood an oil lamp with a conical lampshade made of glass that was green like a billiard cloth. Mr. Dudron recalled that while his father spoke, he sat in the crook of a couch, looking at the king's portrait, which was fading into the shadows and seemed to be slowly erasing itself, disappearing into the immense night of history and of time. Outside you could hear the mournful howl of the storm's wind approaching from the nearby mountains. Beaten by the wind, the branches of the eucalyptus in the garden knocked against the windows' glass.

Mr. Dudron returned to reality. A violent flash of lightning revealed a hill, a lake, and a town. He brightened, thinking that the end of their mad race was near and his fears and anxieties were about to end. After passing through the lacustrine city, the car began to climb a hill. Mr. Dudron was calmer. The lady at the wheel pointed out a villa with a garden; in that villa there had lived and worked a famous novelist whose statue stood in front of the lake in the town's piazza. In the room where the novelist had worked everything remained untouched: the table where he wrote, his inkstand and his pens, his armchair, his library, even the smallest knickknacks that had been there at the moment of his death. He had died while working on his last book, which remained unfinished. One spring morning, the old housekeeper who worked for him entered his study and found him with his head on the table as though he were sleeping; outside the birds twittered and the flowering trees sent out their sweet smells. In the town they say that after the novelist's death the old housekeeper had recounted, talking with her neighbors, that the night before her employer's last breaths she had dreamed she saw him sleeping, seated in his armchair with his head resting on the table, precisely as she found him the next day. They say, too, that on the day of his death, even though no fire had been lit in the house, pure white smoke issued from a chimney, rising and disappearing into the blue. The locals believe it was the spirit of the novelist that vanished like that into the sky.

Climbing, the car's velocity had slowed considerably. This made Mr. Dudron more optimistic. Finally, they stopped in front of a building that gleamed white in the darkness. One or two windows in the mezzanine were illuminated. Suddenly, Mr. Dudron became aware of an inn and, flanking it, a little grocery. He had the impression, too, that one might be able to find lodging there for the night. This last impression was offered by his subconscious in order to reassure him; in truth there was nothing to suggest that the house rented rooms to travelers. However, trusting the impression his subconscious provided, Mr. Dudron reasoned that, if, when he reassumed his seat in the car to return home, he were to experience a sudden weakness, discomfort followed by gastric upset caused by the fear of reexperiencing the panic and excitement that had already rocked him, making it impossible for him to leave, he might find there a room that probably wouldn't provide all the desired comforts but into which he would be able to double-lock himself. He would find a bed that maybe wouldn't be very comfortable but where he nonetheless might, at length, lie down and rest.

They entered through the shop, and immediately a strong odor of laundry soap mixed with rancid pig fat struck Mr. Dudron unpleasantly. Still, the soap smell reminded him that he didn't have any left at home, and so, right then and there, he bought some bathroom soap scented with eau de cologne, for which he paid a trifle. Notwithstanding the modesty of the price and the insignificance of the item, the salesclerk served him with great ceremony; with great care he wrapped the soap in beautiful colored paper, tied it, and handed it to Mr. Dudron with such deference and respectful courtesy that the maestro suddenly felt great embarrassment and at the same time great pity and tenderness for the seller. He would have liked to embrace him and cry with him, to replace the humble shop with a vast and luxurious business where he might have paid large sums for important objects that were splendid and expensive. But that was not possible; this was nothing but a fantasy and Mr. Dudron did not persist in imagining such unrealizable things. He entered a room in the inn where a grand rectangular table was already sumptuously laid with a white cloth, glasses, napkins, knives, and forks. Not far from that grand table, like a foal beside its mare, was another, smaller table covered with bottles of different heights. There were two-liter bottles filled with local wine that, because of their size, dominated the others like Achilles, son of Peleus, and Ajax, son of Telamon, dominated the other Greek heroes in the siege of Troy. This consoling vision was good for Mr. Dudron; he felt, despite everything, optimism stir once more within him; he felt blossoming in his soul a new security, a kind of tranquil joy. Yet, as destiny never offers joy that is pure and without affliction, as soon as he sat at the table, Mr. Dudron realized with a start that it had been set for thirteen. Thirteen at the table and a storm growled in the air. This was the last straw. Mr. Dudron, who had just sat down, got up with savage energy. No, a hundred times no, a thousand times no. With those sinister omens he refused categorically to take part in the meal. He would have sooner retraced on foot those fifty kilometers that separated him from his house; yes, he would have departed alone in the deep night, alone on the deserted street lashed with wind, alone under the threat of imminent hurricane, alone.... But here remorse lodged in his throat and heart; he saw at the other end of the table the surprised and worried faces of the lady who had brought him there in her car and of the industrialist, breeder of snails. This sight made him waver; he was about to sit back down when a providential waiter, more psychologist than he seemed, rescued the situation by bringing over another table, smaller than the first, where settings were placed in a hurry and where Mr. Dudron took his place with two other guests who, out of discretion, joined him so as to prevent the ridiculous appearance that he was being punished. The meal was epically bountiful. The snail eaters were provided with those tiny pliers that make one think of minuscule obstetric instruments, which produced in Mr. Dudron a dreadful impression. More than ever he felt in himself doubts growing about the intelligence and sensitivity of men in general and of his contemporaries in particular. He did not touch the snails despite the encouragements lavished upon him by the other guests who, not content to flaunt the delicate flavor of those mollusks, also spoke to him about their therapeutic qualities, above all for illnesses of the respiratory tract. Serving the table, the waiters joined the conversation, and one of them recounted how a local girl with consumption who had tried every remedy in vain was finally cured completely by not eating anything other than snails stuffed with chopped onions for two straight months. But Mr. Dudron remained steadfast. He ate a leg of roast chicken after an appetizer of prosciutto and sardines in oil. He also requested a plate of buttered spinach, and for dessert, an omelet without salt, abundantly seasoned with strawberry jam; he washed everything down with a glass of house wine. Having finished eating, he removed his pipe, his pouch of tobacco, and a book of Swedish matches from his trouser pocket. Carefully, he filled his pipe and lit it and thus prepared to digest his meal in peace, anticipating a well-deserved repose. But he hadn't taken into account the will and activity—as inexhaustible as it was useless—of the others. All the guests had already risen from the table and with the industrialist at their helm, were getting ready to go out and see the famous breeding grounds. He had to resign himself. Mr. Dudron emptied his pipe into an ashtray and placed it, along with the pouch and the matches, back into his pocket; he buttoned his jacket, and, attempting to make the best of a bad situation, followed the other guests. Outside it was as dark as the inside of an oven. Lightning streaked across the sky and opened breaches, fissures, and cracks of livid light. Holding hands, the guests advanced laboriously, plunging their feet into the soft earth and stumbling over stones and tree roots like the blind men in Brueghel's famous painting. The storm neared, menacing; large, warm drops fell with dull thuds on the soil and on the plants. The wind passed in gusts. Mr. Dudron lifted his head and looked up toward the clouds, which formed a vault that was low and dark. He saw Aeolus and Boreas flying side by side, arms around each other's waists like two figures in a Michelangelo fresco. They puffed out their cheeks like grotesque fountain masks and blew down on the earth and its people their never satisfied wrath.

"Here we are!" he heard someone shout suddenly from the head of the company.

Finally they had arrived at the famous breeding grounds. The guests became agitated; some demanded flashlights, others contented themselves with lighting matches. But the matches blew out as soon as they were lit, and as for flashlights, none had been provided.

"There's one," shouted a guest who had seen, or thought he had seen, a snail.

"There are two," exclaimed another.

Despite his laudable efforts, Mr. Dudron did not manage to make out even a single snail.

Meanwhile, it had begun to rain in earnest. They beat a retreat; the human chain dissolved as each person tried to reach the inn as quickly as possible. They kept sinking into puddles of water. It was worse than a retreat—it was a disaster. Mr. Dudron suddenly found himself near the car, next to the Valkyrie. She got behind the wheel, Mr. Dudron settled himself as best he could into the automobile, and they took off at full speed. The sky's floodgates had opened: the wind had dropped, and long, luminous cords, perfectly perpendicular, united the sky and the land. The rain fell without respite; the land seemed to be boiling. By the time they passed the town on the lake the roads had been transformed into torrents. The car's tires were sunk to their midpoints in water. Not a single passerby. The lady at the wheel had lost her bearings; she did not know which road to take. In vain, she stopped in front of a house with its shutters closed tight, knocking and calling out like a Tyrolean hunter; she was almost a knight errant seeking shelter from a stormy night before a castle with its drawbridge raised. Nobody answered. The only sounds were the continual rumble of the storm and the pounding of water coming down in every direction. Once more, anxiety seized Mr. Dudron; cataclysms flashed into his mind, recollections of tremendous floods in California or China of which he once saw shocking scenes reproduced in an illustrated magazine. He imagined the town swept away by the water and submerged in the lake; quadrupeds, oxen, horses fighting the currents; women in nightgowns, their hair disheveled, holding a child in one arm while clinging with the other to shutters or to the balconies of half-submerged houses. He saw seminude men on rooftops lowering poles and throwing ropes to the unfortunates floundering in the water. Then he saw the lake overflowing its banks, expanding across the plain and reaching, in the end, in that other city, his house, where he jealously guarded his paintings, his books, his memories, everything he loved and without which he would not be able to live. Such horror!

Suddenly the lady let out a squeal of joy—she had seen a road sign! They had to turn left, then right, and then left once more, and they would be on the main road. They made it out of the town. Their speed increased. Mr. Dudron noticed with pleasure that as they got farther from the lake and the mountains, the rain lessened. After a few kilometers he felt it wasn't raining anymore; he looked out the window and up and saw the stars. "Probably the mountains—especially that one they call the Great Saw, so much taller than the others—cause the storms to develop," thought Mr. Dudron. Now he was feeling completely reassured; despite the speed of the car, everything seemed to him secure and calm, and so he was moved to reflect on the relativity of things. They passed once more through the little town with its monument in memory of the king's assassination, but this time something else stirred feelings in Mr. Dudron that were powerful, profound, and strange. Passing a piazza surrounded by porticoes surmounted by houses whose blinds were all closed, the car's headlights illuminated violently and for an instant a large basin, in the middle of which a tall jet of spurting water stood out like a large white spot. The sight of that fountain, which—in the middle of a deserted piazza in that deeply sleeping town immersed in darkness, gloom, and solitude—continued to spurt, to shoot its jets of water in profusion into the air and to raise its song in the profound night, awoke in Mr. Dudron strange and highly metaphysical feelings. He suddenly felt immense pity for the fountain and even a sort of shame for having to speed past and abandon it once more to silence, solitude, and darkness. He should have just stopped the car right here, woken everyone up, had them ring the bells, carry torches, light all the lights, string venetian lamps from the porticoes, hang tapestries and streamers from the balconies and the windows, tie garlands, invite musicians with their instruments, strike up the dances, open barrels of wine, fill the piazza with celebrating people—that is, done *something* so that the poor fountain would not remain spurting and singing alone in the great desolation and silence of the night. But the car passed quickly, and with a tug at his heart Mr. Dudron watched the fountain sink and disappear into the dark.

A short time later he arrived. Quite pleased to find himself once more at home, Mr. Dudron said good night to the lady, thanked her, and went inside. Notwithstanding the sustained exertion, he did not feel like sleeping. He opened the window and leaned out; he looked up into the great night. Numerous stars sparkled against the background of a sky black like ink. Some sparkled in groups, others in a line or alone, well-spaced. Mr. Dudron thought about the futility of his sacrifices, the debts he hadn't settled, his jeopardized situation. Instead of moaning and sinking into pessimistic reflections about destiny and humankind, he remembered those early days when he had realized how to revitalize not just *his own painting*, but *Painting* as a whole. Enormous pride mixed with the sweetest memories engulfed him. He saw once more the scenes captured by his first works in the new style. Yes, he was seeing these places once more: the valley stretching far in the sweet light of the September sun. In the far ground a stream flowed, winding. Boulders of red earth rose here and there, and larger rocks appeared in the distance like cliffs jutting out over the countryside that was covered with mature grain and flecked with red poppies. Ahead, on a hill, the vegetation was so abundant and the trees so dense they covered the houses and small villas almost entirely. To the right, the composition of a farmstead seemed painted on a theater set. Ridge-tiled roofs suggested a working farm. A house, its facade adorned with columns, was centered against the background of a forest and a meadow that receded to the shore, where a line of poplars was reflected in the water. "Memories!" thought Mr. Dudron. And completely swept up in his reveries, he continued to look up at the stars. A streak of luminous atmospheric dust extended from north to south, forking above his head. Between these glimmers there were large empty spaces, and the sky seemed a vast sea of the most profound blue, with archipelagos, islands, and islets. He remembered something he once heard: behind the Milky Way there are nebulas; on the other side of the nebulas there are stars and more stars without number, of which the nearest is separated from us by three hundred billion myriameters. He turned toward Ursa Major, which he had always loved; he looked for the North Star and then Cassiopeia and her constellation. At the same time, Mr. Dudron continued to think and talk to himself: "So, one must summon a past that, apparently, should no longer have to appear upon the stage of memory. Using actions that have been around for years and that have allowed the real culprits to perform despicable acts, one must go ahead with various investigations—in the realm of Order as well as in the direction of that *other* shore, where we all seek recompense for our exhausting, even dangerous work."

Suddenly, Mr. Dudron felt a great shudder pass through his body. "Pneumonia," he thought with anxiety, and he saw himself prostrated by the illness, cared for by indifferent people. He was afraid. He reentered the house, closed the windows, and drew the shades. He lay down after taking care to place all of his garments except for his overcoat on his bed to make it warmer. He also added an old ink-stained cloth that he kept on a table and upon which could be distinguished embroidery representing Hindu warriors who brandished torches and drove elephants before them. He added a few old newspapers that he found at the bottom of a drawer. He lay down, and immediately the heat of the bed heartened him. He looked at a painting on an easel illuminated feebly by a candle on his bedside table. This painting, which he had finished some days prior, depicted an ancient beach with a tranquil and solemn beauty. The sky was yellow-orange and reflected in the sea. The horizon was indicated with a line of flaming red. In the sky a few little clouds, whose roundness was shaped by violet shadows, drifted, scattering like lambs at pasture. From the height of a rock jutting out over the sea, a sanctuary made a white spot. On the beach in the foreground, among some broken column fragments that attested with their presence to the transience of human constructions, was a group: a young warrior held the reins of a large white horse whose immense tail spilled to the ground like an avalanche, strong and rippling. On the other side an old athlete, a kind of Hercules at rest, leaned on a rock and gazed across the sea with a pensive air.

"That's it," thought Mr. Dudron, "what today most pleases those concerned with painting, the intellectuals and the pederasts. For them painting is merely a question of images. In the history of art, our age will certainly be remembered for the ignorance of those concerned with painting. They don't understand that images mean absolutely nothing and the only thing that saves a painting from oblivion, that makes it valuable, that renders it immortal, is *its quality*. But let's put aside," he continued, "these thorny questions that only time can resolve and plunge back into the metaphysical question, not to appease a certain class of our contemporaries, but because this aspect of art attracts us as much as the other.

"As for the painting in front of me, perhaps it is the memory of a past life that is now, in the eternal present, bound to my life. A memory of what was and an expectation of what will be, lazy or strenuous vigils and you, my good sleep, who takes me sweetly every night into your arms! You, my good sleep, heavy and slow like a great river! The wave where I will rest definitively nears, from age to age..."

Mr. Dudron's eyelids became heavy; it took effort to keep them open. So he blew out his candle, stretched himself voluptuously beneath his covers and, after turning over two or three times, fell into a profound sleep. And he dreamed.

It was still night, but the stars had disappeared. Mr. Dudron found himself in a park or public garden of unprecedented romanticism and banality. There were monuments of marble and bronze representing sages, politicians, and generals who had served science or the nation. The sages and politicians were almost always sitting in an armchair with a pensive expression, holding a book or roll of paper in their hands. The soldiers, erect on their feet with swords in their hands, looked straight ahead into the distance; at their feet were smashed cannons and balls arranged in pyramids. Ivy climbed around them; there were also succulent plants, ruins, shrines, moss, and grottoes. In another part, bridges, tiny and rustic, were cast over brooks that murmured over grasses and pebbles. A kind of Rialto climbed a dock whose edges were encrusted with snails. Along the shady and deserted paths of this park Mr. Dudron strolled slowly, hugging and pressing to his breast a child with a melancholy and intelligent look. She was the daughter of the woman he loved. "This is her daughter!" thought Mr. Dudron in his dream, and this thought flooded his heart with infinite sweetness. In the dream, the landscapes he had loved reappeared to his memory. Dream or reality, everything was there, everything. Toys taken out of cardboard boxes; toys painted and sparkling, scattered across the dining room table during winter evenings when outside the snow places little white caps everywhere and the bells announce the coming holidays. Little toy soldiers of colored lead; tiny houses, neater than anything; crèches and ships on rollers.

All palpable and conveyable joy, every guarantee of joy that the very gods, yes, even those sweetest gods with silky blond beards and eyes that squint ineffably, those same gods with distant expressions who smile without comprehension, those gods that ultimately don't know anything for the simple reason that *there is nothing to know*, yes, the joy that those gods, too, are reluctant to give. Before placing their absolutely illegible signatures at the bottom of those solemn papers endorsed by Destiny and stamped by Eternity, they twirl and chew their mustaches with a preoccupied air and clench their jaws beneath their beards. But once you have this paper you may rest easy and for a long time. Mr. Dudron knew this as he knew he was dreaming. It was not, therefore, any surprise when he realized that the child had disappeared and the scene had shifted completely. Arborescent boxwoods whose bitter scent was exacerbated by the heat were the only ornament in a shadowy and humid gorge where the raging water of the cold torrents murmured, sonorous. And then, all of a sudden, an oasis. The horizon had widened. Large trees interlaced their leafy branches playing ring-around-the-rosy on the green meadow where the river, finally coming to its senses, showed off its silver garlands. In this unexpected landscape, near a small waterfall that seemed to spring from a rock, there was an altar, a block of white marble with a cloth of the softest yellow-orange covering it and falling to the floor in classical folds; at the foot of the altar roses and laurel wreaths were scattered. Mr. Dudron's mother was there, looking like she had when she was young. She was seated upon the tender grass in a tranquil and resigned posture of prayer and meditation. She was very beautiful; she looked like a woman from the Bible. In the sky a clear dawn illuminated the world with a diffuse light from which the shadows had vanished. Mr. Dudron, advancing laboriously as though his feet were blocks, wanted to approach his mother, but the scene changed yet again. It was midday. The sun shone upon a field covered with yellow grain. In the distance the bonnet of a carriage slid slowly by. A torpor spread through the air. No song of any bird, no buzz of any insect.

"I have returned by tortuous paths," thought Mr. Dudron in the dream while he considered the new landscape. "I have returned on paths where sharp pebbles, brambles, and thorns are not lacking. Ah me! I have returned to this stage of life I abandoned many years ago. I concerned myself with mountains and with beaches, with lines tracing seashores, with the anatomy of branches that vary from tree to tree, with the colors of the sky that change according to the hour, the weather, and the season. I believed that these figures posed the most varied, most numerous, most complicated, and most thrilling problems. Only—that's it—it is still necessary to think of other things. To avoid being oppressed, or even bothered, in order for your thoughts to remain natural, you need not shine too bright a light. Often, life's necessities are in direct opposition to those sometimes numerous necessities of the environment in which you'd like to operate, work, think, create, relax, rest, have fun—live! You must prepare a very precise and particular dosage from the different wells where your own inspirations are drawn. I know the joy of discovery and the bitterness of disappointment! Yes, I remember well that clear and long-ago winter day. An immense torpor weighed upon me; the horizon of an inconceivable purity shined with eternity's light, and at the harbor, the shadows of the ships' masts, and of the smokestacks stretched up to the houses, up to the offices of the great shipping companies, up to the warehouses from which emanated the smell of leather, tar, and smoked fish."

Thus, Mr. Dudron spoke to himself in his dream, and in the meantime his dread, along with the upset stomach he had been feeling up until that moment, dissipated completely, yielding to a sensation of tranquility and security. It was, therefore, without emotion that he found himself suddenly involved in a bear hunt in the depths of a forest. "Warning," said a voice near him, "the beast is merely wounded. It will charge the hunter!"

He had just heard this sentence in his dream when a gunshot resounded and Mr. Dudron woke up. He stretched, yawned, looked for his watch, and saw that it was 10:00 a.m. "It was my neighbor's son," exclaimed Mr. Dudron, "who woke me up again, doing target practice with his carbine in the garden."

Thinking about his neighbor's son, he remembered with sadness his own adopted son, his Bruno, the youngster who was so dear to him and for whom he and his wife had made so many sacrifices, even during the most difficult moments of their lives. They had hoped these sacrifices would one day bear fruit; they had hoped that when Bruno became an adolescent they might steer him toward the study of law or mathematics, make a lawyer of him or an engineer, a man above all honest and also serious and hardworking. But, alas, entering Bruno's room with his wife one morning to bring him his hot chocolate, Mr. Dudron found the little bed empty and the sailor suit left out on a chair. A letter, placed conspicuously on the mantelpiece, explained everything: "I am leaving," the letter read, "because there is more for me out there. I am returning your sailor outfit, whose coarse wool has made me suffer cruelly as though a necklace and bracelets made of nettles surrounded my neck and wrists. I don't need these clothes anymore because with the money I was given I've bought myself some magnificent sportswear: a golf cap and triple-soled shoes reinforced with rubber."

Someone—and it was always him: that immensely rich shipowner with the long face and short, doggish legs who had seduced and thrust their Bruno toward flight, their dear boy! In a postscript to the letter the prodigal son added that "someone has offered the use of a villa."

Yes, their dove had flown. Like a coward, treacherously he had flown. The years had passed, more or less sad, more or less gay, as all years pass. Now, down in the great city, white and solemn, where the militarized and uncompromising tribunes kept watch in their severe, black uniforms, grown Bruno, successful Bruno leaned out under the vault of vast cupolas to listen to the sonorous and polyphonic waves that climbed and climbed without rest from the melogenic caverns, from the caverns where formidable orchestras took shelter in tight and disciplined ranks, directed by conductors with thick, ruffled heads of hair who, with horrendous grimaces and epileptic gestures, pushed ever higher the sublimity of the great unfinished symphonies.

Mr. Dudron thought of his prodigal child, but without hate or wrath. "After all," he said to himself, "every man for himself is the law that rules the world." At the same time, he chided himself for having more than once *missed his chance*. He looked at his room, brightened by the light of day, and thought of his dreams from the night before and of his adventures of the past evening. "It is mysterious, this life that begins again each morning," he said to himself. He knew that upon rising he was supposed to ensure the essential security of a well-trimmed, well-shod, and well-dressed man who feels his interior jacket pocket buttoned around his wallet, a wallet that he knows to be supplied with large bills and checks to cash, with identity cards and passports perfectly in order. What is more, this man knows that in the other pockets of his clothing he'll find everything necessary, no, indispensable to a prudent person, healthy in body and mind, when he leaves his residence to venture into that forest—always mysterious and full of surprises—that is the modern city: a fountain pen, a journal for lists and addresses, penknife, a wooden tube containing tincture of iodine, a small bandage roll, watch and compass, pocket comb, pencil with point protector, booklet for notes, a metal box with at least six tablets for occasional headaches, a pouch of tobacco devotedly refilled, pipe, matches, a small piece of rusty metal or coral horn to touch at the passing of a funeral procession or an individual with a reputation for the evil eye or in general when in the presence of anyone or thing prone to bringing bad luck.

Having consulted his watch, Mr. Dudron realized that it was past time to get dressed and go out. Yes, to go out, but go where? All this was no longer sufficient to calm his spirit, which had grown bucolic and tolerant only by great force. As far as *city outings* went, he knew by now what to stick to. He was familiar with these great centers where the mechanical instincts of millions and millions of his kind converged and where, night and day, a crowd exasperated by the battle for life clamored beneath harmonious groups sculpted in marble and obscured in the fog and smoke, which, on their cube-shaped pedestals, represented music, dance, thought, and poetry. "Being satisfied with oneself," thought Mr. Dudron, "is not everything. One must further achieve that series of small victories that secure our position in life and raise bulwarks around us, indispensable for protecting us against the attacks that our peers, whoever they may be, sooner or later direct against us. Of course, there's nature. Nature!..." In Mr. Dudron's mind the sound of this word evoked visions that were less than reassuring. He saw before him deserted beaches and milky, tremendously tranquil seas. At the horizon, a sun—red and tragically solitary disk—set slowly amidst the mists. "A smoking horizon," thought Mr. Dudron. A monstrous animal with the head of a parrot, an enormous black mass like a mountain, emerged slowly from the water and dragged itself across the sand through the shells, some of which moved a bit, struggled to shift position, then fell flat and remained still. Then there were tranquil and gloomy lakes surrounded by dark fir trees. In the distance, tall mountains raised peaks whose long crevices were full of snow. From the summit of one rock a waterfall plunged into a lake. Though this waterfall was very far away, its thundering reached all the way to Mr. Dudron, so still was the air and complete the silence.

Mr. Dudron remained lost in thought and indecisive. "Ultimately," he said to himself, "all of this pleases me as little as the spectacle of agitated and mechanized cities. It is true that there is also humankind; there is *humanity*: the young seamstress who works long into the night to provide for a feeble father, an elderly mother, young siblings who need clothing and feeding, and for whom one must pay for school. Under lamplight she pushes her needle while her thoughts fly toward her sweetheart, the lover who on Sunday will drive her to the countryside to pick strawberries in the woods and drink fresh milk at the farms. Sometimes, too, there is betrayal and its dramas. The young, unmarried mother who carries her baby in her arms and hides like a hunted beast behind the columns of the church where, just two steps from her, accompanied by the asthmatic chords of the organ playing the wedding march, *he is*—passing all dressed up, freshly shaven with his cheeks powdered, smiling, and with his wife on his arm, *his wife*, dressed in white and crowned with orange blossoms, and behind them the requisite procession of relatives, friends, and invited guests."

Mr. Dudron got up; he put on his slippers and slipped into his dressing gown. His decision was made; it was irrevocable. He sat down in front of his easel, armed himself with his palette and brushes, and, taking up a work that he had sketched out the day before, began, calmly, to paint.

He had been working for some time when there came a knock at the door and a young lady entered. It was Isabella Far, a writer of whom Mr. Dudron often spoke with his friends. She was gifted with a philosophical intelligence, or rather, a philosophical talent unique in the history of women writers. She came often to see Mr. Dudron, whom she considered the sole modern painter to comprehend the mystery of great painting. She thought him the only painter capable of returning fallen painting to a level of nobility and beauty.

"Good afternoon, madam!" said Mr. Dudron, rising and setting down his palette, "I had been hoping to see you because some questions about the problems of painting in general, and the situation of modern painting in particular, have been nagging at my thoughts since this morning. I wonder how you would explain, for example, the mania for intellectualism, the fixation with seeming clever that one finds today among those who are

concerned with art in general and modern art in particular."
Isabella Far collected herself for a moment and then spoke: "In each era one observes a preference for a particular quality, a particular human capacity.

"There have been periods during which what was esteemed above all was courage and the art of making war. In others virtue and abstinence were admired. And in others still, elegance and refinement were placed at the highest level.

"Our age, too, has its ideal, and this ideal is *intelligence*. A great number of our contemporaries desire one thing alone: to be or at least *to seem intelligent*.

"However, given that intelligence is a gift from heaven and cannot be acquired by other means, to substitute they have invented *intellectualism*. While natural gifts are indispensable for intelligence, intellectualism can be learned easily enough! One needs only to have a standard memory, not too much personality, and to follow the current without distrust.

"The phenomenon of modern art is a phenomenon that demonstrates, more than any other, man's need to create intellectualism because real intelligence is becoming ever rarer.

"The docile acceptance of modern painting, sculpture, music, and literature, which our contemporaries display, will remain for future centuries a completely miraculous event."

Mr. Dudron listened to Isabella Far's words with great attention, and again he was struck by her surprising clarity of spirit and crushing logic. He listened to her, smiling with approval. He cast a glance at the painting he had not yet completed and then asked, "How do you explain, madam, you who see all things so clearly, how do you explain the lack of talent and power that is found in art today? How do you explain why there are so few painters who know how to make what is called *a painting*, that is to say, something that stands up and that one can look at with pleasure?"

Once more Isabella Far collected herself for a few moments and answered: "The previous century, especially its first half, gave us masterpieces in all the arts. You would now like to know, Maestro, the causes of modern decadence; you spoke above all of painting because that is the art that interests you most.

"I think that in the last century humankind produced too many artists of genius. A pause was inevitable, and that pause, by coincidence or by the will of nature, coincided with a moment in history during which important social changes took place.

"The aristocrats and other exceptional characters who, in the past, had been the arbiters of the arts were gradually replaced by the bourgeoisie, who began to be the principal art buyers, lovers, and critics.

"But the new patrons could not style themselves as connoisseurs of art. To truly comprehend the worth of a work of art one must have above all a natural artistic sense, and one must then cultivate that sense over a long period. We must before all else have inherited this artistic sensibility from our parents or, better still, from our grandparents. Remember, Mr. Dudron, that to truly comprehend a work of art you need a long tradition or, without it, exceptional intelligence.

"Just as for specialists, long years of experience are necessary to judge a fabric, which is of course a material they can actually touch with their fingers, whose threads they can burn or otherwise experiment on to see if the wool or silk is pure—how many more years must be necessary to judge the quality of a work of art, where only our artistic sensibility and our culture can guide us!"

"It is very right what you say, madam," answered Mr. Dudron, "but how do you explain the absolute lack of craft that rages today; and how do you explain why today even the rare painters with a bit of talent paint badly, why their paintings are made with bad material and, as a result, are of bad quality?"

After having reflected a moment, Isabella Far responded, "Indeed, this progressive and by now long-realized loss of the technical secrets of painting is mysterious. In all ages there have existed and worked second-tier and even mediocre artists, but they all followed, more or less successfully, in the tradition of the great masters. I think that the artists of the last century, finding themselves before a public without culture, abandoned the tradition of great painting that had been upheld through Delacroix and really up to Courbet. These artists abandoned tradition and dedicated themselves to ornamentation; more and more, painting became ornamentation, and ornamentation is what it almost always is today. More often than not, extremely bad ornamentation.

"Decadence began with Manet. Notwithstanding the talent that you can still feel in his works, in his paintings I see the destiny that painting will suffer after him. Later the quality of painting becomes completely subsumed by decoration, by invention, and by false beauty.

"Great painting is beautiful; it has a beauty that is serious and severe; subject and color don't matter. There are masterworks for whose subjects the ancient masters chose old men with wrinkled faces—still the paintings are stupendous, uniting beautiful material and the magnificent execution of genius!

"The pleasure we experience in looking at a masterwork is equal to the pleasure we feel listening to deeply inspired music or reading works of philosophy—in the dawning understanding of a great idea. This pleasure is so precious because it is incited not by human nature's animal instincts but by the comprehension of elevated things of the spirit. It is a pleasure that finds its origin in the Greater Good."

"Wonderful, madam!" exclaimed Mr. Dudron, "I am truly happy to hear such clear, intelligent, and logical ideas. I thank you! I still have many other questions to ask you, but I fear that I will tire you out and so I leave all that to the next time I have the pleasure of seeing you..."

"I am very glad to have been able to enlighten you about certain issues, Maestro," said Isabella Far. "You have done well to defer our philosophical discussions until next time; indeed, I must run, in order to return to work."

Midday only just sounded, Mr. Dudron busied himself with his meal. For economic motives he had rented himself a small, furnished apartment with a kitchen. The apartment was in a building that only rented furnished apartments. Mr. Dudron was very pleased because this way he could easily eat at home. In the hotel where he had lived previously, the restaurant prices were too high for his means, such that he couldn't even manage what they call a half pension.

This is why, for the entirety of his sojourn in the hotel, Mr. Dudron contrived to eat in his room. He purchased provisions in the neighborhood shops. But his great difficulty arose when, heavily burdened with provisions of all kinds, he had to cross the hotel lounge, which was always full of gay, elegant young women and sporty men wearing English fashions. All of these people regularly took their meals in the hotel restaurant, and, while they waited to be seated at their tables, drank costly aperitifs. Mr. Dudron strode through that crowd filled with people who seemed happy and sure of themselves; he strode with a step that he forced himself to render resolute and with the expression of a man whose lofty metaphysical speculations won't permit him to get mixed up in the pleasures and frivolities of his contemporaries. But, to be honest, he knew very well that it rang false. He knew that in the pockets of his trousers, his jacket, and his overcoat, parcels upon parcels were stuffed: there were cans of sardines and tuna, slices of prosciutto and salami, olives, eggs, boiled potatoes, and pastries purchased from the pastrycook, which consisted of a rectangle of bland, half-cooked dough topped with a bit of marmalade as sour as the juice of a lemon. As for bread, it is better not to speak of it—the bread was Mr. Dudron's terror. Those long hunks of bread they call baguettes, which the bakers would half-wrap in a minuscule piece of parchment, were the most difficult thing to hide. Naturally, as soon as he left the bakery Mr. Dudron tried to thrust the baguettes like stakes into the mass of boxes and parcels overflowing his pockets.

When he reentered the hotel loaded down in this way, icy shivers went down his back. He was terrorized by the indiscreet stares unleashed by the staff in the lobby; above all, he feared the glare of the porter, who was covered in stripes like an admiral and severe like a president of the Supreme Court of Cassation. Mr. Dudron breathed again only when, after having reached his room on the top floor, he could lock himself in and, emptying upon the table the contents of his pockets, fall into the single armchair, his forehead awash in cold sweat.

But all this was now long past. His terrors had disappeared and with them his angst and shame. Almost all the tenants of this building were people without servants who, as a result, went themselves to do their shopping. All of these people returned laden with provisions. Some tenants, especially certain white-haired intellectuals with American glasses, were more discreet than others and carried their provisions in leather bags, even small valises.

Now Mr. Dudron knew that he no longer had any reason to feel embarrassed and terrorized, and he experienced a fierce joy in returning home with his arms full of packages and big loaves that he no longer made any effort to hide; once he even came in with a gigantic squash under his arm. His attitude was now truly and sincerely calm and secure when he passed before the doorman to reenter his apartment. Though he was laden with every kind of provision, he walked with his head high and his eyes straight ahead, as a wife in an advanced state of pregnancy walks, leaning on the arm of her legitimate consort on a nice Sunday afternoon.

Yes: to walk with head high, eyes ahead, through a crowd of his contemporaries—that was what Mr. Dudron wanted. But his contemporaries, because they were hysterical or in order to irritate him, pretended not to notice anything and completely ignored the enormous distance that existed between him and them. As such, Mr. Dudron was almost always at a disadvantage in these sorts of encounters, but he didn't dare admit or fully recognize it and lost himself in all kinds of theories and internal discussions to prove to himself that in the final tally the winner was himself.

Since Mr. Dudron was one of those men whose life flowed, cradled each day by the melancholy music of remembrance, he saw in his memory the autumn moon of a humid autumn evening some years back; that moon rose slowly in the cloudy sky behind the church bell towers. Leaves the color of leather and rust fell from the plane trees and chestnut trees; they came down twirling and then dragged in the damp dirt of the trails and roads. Men in secondhand overcoats returned home without conviction, and shopkeepers, after a day of meager business, lowered the rolling shutters of their stores with the sound of a rifle discharging. A murmuring, confused and indefinable, came from every place and repeated insistently in Mr. Dudron's ear that *everything is in vain*. "Nevertheless," he thought as he scraped the bowl of his pipe, "nevertheless I will never forget that wild place where my father would take me and my brother to walk in the days of our youth. It was a small promontory a few kilometers away from the city where we lived, upon which rested one of the arches of the old bridge tossed across the river's estuary.

"The promontory held a meadow where there flowered many white daisies, poppies, and other wildflowers, which threw a polychrome mantle over that piece of earth. Butterflies of varied hues flew from one flower to another. Below the promontory's nearest arch, the water, closed in, frothed and seemed to boil. Into a crack in one of the old blackened stones of the bridge the wind had blown a hawthorn seed; the seed had found within that crack a bit of earth that had been gathering there maybe for more than a century; mosses of various sizes, nourished by the humidity of the nude rock, had sprouted in succession, and each little plant, dying after having lived its mossy life, had become a bit of earth sufficient for a larger moss. Finally, at the end, among those innumerable seeds the crazy wind carries whimsically across space, there appeared a hawthorn seed; maybe it had even fallen from the beak of a bird who made its nest in some hole in the bridge and who was bringing its hungry babies some of those red seed balls that had remained on the hawthorn through spring. The seed had become a thick and robust plant; its roots, climbing, had gone searching all around for other cracks where a bit of earth could be found. The hawthorn hung from the top of the bridge in long garlands that moved unceasingly even in the gentlest breeze, and which were wetted by sprays of water. At the end of May and for a part of June, these garlands were covered in small petals of light pink which, as they lived their little lives, loosened, fell into the river, and, transported along the foamy waters, slipped away and disappeared."

This long soliloquy had tired Mr. Dudron out. Nevertheless, he was content, with a contentment veiled in melancholy. During sad moments it was his habit to recall a memory from his long-ago childhood. He had the impression the memory might illuminate many mysteries for him. His richly artistic, impassioned, ardent, and religious nature delighted in this particularly. And with this recollection, others returned to his memory. Recollections of landscapes, yes, but where had he seen those landscapes?... In what moment of his adventurous, arduous, and complicated life?... They were impossible to remember precisely, but they were landscapes nevertheless. Landscapes! Mr. Dudron loved landscapes, real ones as much as painted ones. He loved the landscapes of the great masters, above all those of Rubens, where the air circulates through the leaves of the trees and the clouds navigate the spaces of the sky. He held therefore in horror the landscapes of the modern school because he found them to be painted badly, without talent, somehow muddy and flat. Now he saw passing, as across the backdrop of a theater set, these landscapes; oh, how he saw them! He even saw typical landscapes, perfectly anonymous and rooted in tens, hundreds of exemplars in a region's registries. Some seemed carved out of the flat surface of the countryside; others slept in the sweet harmony of the knolls amid the gray of the rural houses. Elsewhere you could see brown rectangles of worked earth, the alternating green of the meadows, the fresh varnish of those expanses of land planted with beetroot that have now taken hold in all climates. Here and there darker clusters, streaked with rust by autumn, broke off with their irregular forms in the middle of that powerful scene of rural riches, which the quotidian labor of the farmer had measured with a heavy and resigned step for centuries. And then there were the woods: groups of birches created a miniature oasis amid the fields of grain and were useful to hunters for ambushes, before the real forest out there, the gloomy and humid forest, held and maintained with no expense spared to provide to the whole estate the reserves of meat from a double-barreled shotgun....

Mr. Dudron loved landscapes and observed nature. Every once in a while he would pick up stones or pebbles and gaze steadily at them, rotating them to all sides. Then he would place them on a table and, picking up pencil and paper, copy them patiently, adjusting the light. Drawn on the paper, those stones and those pebbles would then take on the look of wild, deserted sites, of rocky mountains and cliffs overhanging an imaginary sea. Mostly he made these drawings in the evening. He would place the stone and pebble perpendicular to the lamplight to achieve contrast and effects of the light, and then, drawing, he imagined it was high noon in a rocky and wild place in the time of the Greek myths. He would imagine the sun at the apex of its journey and its rays, falling, descending like lead upon the earth. They conjured sublime moments, all resonant with sweet eternity, when profound notes from Pan's flute, hidden in thickets of reeds, wafted solemn and consoling in the tepid and unmoving air. In his mind, Mr. Dudron conjured those mountains at midday in happy times; he saw grottoes inhabited by centaur families. He saw the centauride stretched out in the sun at the entrance of the cavern, about to nurse her young. Since their human-horse nature was split equally and symmetrically, she offered, alternating, now her mother's breast, now her mare's teat. Centaur-colts toddled joyfully around, chasing each other and offering up joyful yells in which the whinny of the young horse was blurred with the shrill cry of the adolescent, intoxicated with space and freedom. Meanwhile, the centaur, head of the family, went off to hunt with his bow and quiver full of arrows. Lying in ambush behind a rock or a shrub, he patiently awaited the passage of some large-winged creature or wild boar. Sometimes he even gathered acorns, blackberries, and herbs. In the evening, after returning to his grotto, he would roast the game, skewered on a long, sharpened branch. He would crush acorns and grind them between two flat rocks.

When the sky darkened and the owls aroused the mountain's echoes with their mournful cries and the bats began to emerge and descend into the dusk with their drunk birds' flight, like the arms of an enormous pendulum, then the whole centaur family retired to the depths of the grotto after obstructing the entrance with a great mass of rock, whose budging required the centaur, centauride, and their children to combine their efforts.

Sometimes Mr. Dudron would hold a rock against the light. Then he would see a mountain behind which the sun had set. The summit's irregular profile stood out sharply against the sky still lit up by the dying star. All these sketches were very suggestive and evocative, and Mr. Dudron loved to show them now and then to his friends, who would emit cries of admiration even if, after all, they felt no pleasure viewing them and understood absolutely nothing. "Everything is around us and near us," Mr.

Dudron used to say, "every thing, even the most unlikely. The most fabulous monsters are here, steps away. Look, for example, at the lizard that slides along the wall of your garden and stops where the wall is hottest, exposed longest to the scorching rays of the summer sun. That lizard is the dragon of myth, of religion, and of legends. It is the dragon slain by Saint George, master of the Spirit of Evil; the dragon pierced by the sword of Perseus, who freed the beautiful Andromeda; the dragon decapitated by Ruggiero to save Angelica. These are mysteries, my dear friends, mysteries like the sounds that furniture sometimes makes in the great silence of the late night."

Meanwhile Mr. Dudron sought to amuse himself, to dispel that vague tedium, that indefinable melancholy that undermined his sensitive spirit. He tried to amuse himself by philosophizing and observing the things and men around him. As for his observation of men, the situation wasn't as interesting as he might have hoped. In that immense pavilion surrounded by enormous windows like an aquarium, women of a certain age, their heads uncovered, passed and repassed, and Mr. Dudron could not manage to explain the true reason for all that movement. On metal chairs men sat skimming newspapers with tired and skeptical expressions while the hems of their overcoats trailed sadly in the dust on the ground. Other women, seated here and there, were busy sewing or mending linens. They talked among themselves in quiet voices, as though in church. Children passed, hurling sharp shouts, or, bending their knees and squeezing their elbows to their sides, they advanced with tiny steps, dragging their feet on the ground and shaping their mouths into small funnels from which bubbles of saliva burst while they emitted sounds that imitated jets of steam from a locomotive set in motion.

Mr. Dudron had a horror of children. He could never comprehend what took place in the souls and spirits of those whose faces shone whenever they found themselves in the presence of a child—those beings full of malice, with sly or completely stupid and brutish expressions, those beings who smell of urine and saliva, who look at you with vitreous eyes beneath craniums that are soft and red like cooked shrimp. Children didn't just inspire a sacred horror in him, they terrorized him too.

"Why," Mr. Dudron asked himself, "is there such a difference between human children and the children of other animals?... Take, for example, a lion cub, a small tiger, a small elephant, a puppy, a kitten, a colt, even a chick: how good they are, how kind, cordial, spontaneous, joyous, affable, and grateful; one feels real pleasure in petting and touching them. As soon as you show them a little bit of interest they are immediately content and ready to play with you, but without malice, without suspicion and hostility, and without arriving, in their play, at those hysterical and naughty excesses of humankind's young. When you try to be courteous to a child, what happens? He looks at you with his wicked criminal's gaze without responding to your overtures; or he throws himself upon you, trying by all means to annoy you, to paralyze your movements and even make you ridiculous, especially if there are others present at the scene."

Now it happened that when Mr. Dudron spoke of the antipathy children provoked in him, people would invariably say, "But dear Mr. Dudron, you speak this way because you have never had children, as a result you cannot understand certain feelings. If you had had children, you would have loved them as you love the young of other animals. After all, you would have been an excellent family man; one can see from your face that you are a good man, sweet and sentimental."

These conversations never convinced Mr. Dudron, and the fact of having the air of a good, sweet, and sentimental man gratified his self-respect only to a point. He would have preferred hearing that he had the face of a pirate or a bandit.

"It's true," thought Mr. Dudron, "one shouldn't complicate one's life with such problems, investing all one's self-respect in the desire to have the face of a buccaneer. It ends up degenerating into hysterical mania. I know that man fears and is ashamed of being seen in a state of weakness and powerlessness—this is the reason why a normal man is ashamed to be seen by a woman in bed, especially if she is young. You mustn't assume that his shame and embarrassment are linked to the fact that he is nude or seminude in bed, because generally a man in bed is even more covered than a man dressed and on his feet. It's just that a man lying in bed, below the sheets and covers, evokes the idea of powerlessness, not because he makes you think of a sick man but more because the scene suggests the idea of a man restrained, of a man who is not free in his movements, of a man who, if necessary, would not be able to defend himself or whomever needed defending—yes, therefore, in my opinion, a man in bed suggests the idea of powerlessness."

On the subject of misconstrued self-respect, he was about to recount to himself the curious story of a painter friend of his when he saw passing at some distance Isabella Far, she of the philosophical intelligence, and he ran to catch up with her because he still wanted to know some things and to clarify several questions regarding modern painting. After the standard pleasantries and once Isabella Far had agreed to linger for a moment, they headed toward a little-frequented street and sat down on a park bench. "How do you explain, madam," asked Mr. Dudron, "the appearance of art dealers and the part they have played in this last part of the century?"

After reflecting for a few moments, Isabella Far responded, "I believe, Maestro, that the great interest displayed by the Jewish people for that which is called modern painting is due to the fact that they love abstraction and everything to which it is connected; on the other hand, they don't love concrete creation. They are a people who never desired to see the divine image translated into reality, perhaps fearing so to diminish the abstract side of the idea of God. Other peoples have felt the basic need to be able to touch, embrace, or, at least, admire the image of their gods or their God. From this need to represent the Lord in the most perfect and ideal manner, art was born, and true art is indeed a parcel of the divine spirit living among us.

"The bourgeoisie constituted a public less elite than aristocrats and other eminent persons, but on the other hand, they were more numerous. Buyers of art, no experts, felt the need to be guided in their choices, *and thus appeared art dealers.*

"This designation, *art dealer*, is very apt for designating men who weren't really lovers or enthusiasts of art, but simply merchants who wanted to sell their wares. As a result, art dealers played an important part in the ignorance and decadence of painting."

"What you are saying, madam, is truly very interesting and above all intelligent and correct. I too have observed all of this, but had not managed to formulate my thoughts in a manner so clear, so precise, and also so philosophically logical as you have just done."

"Then I will continue," resumed Isabella Far, "and I will tell you something more about the origins and causes of the lamentable conditions in which painting struggles nowadays. We must not forget that the public was tired of excessive sweetness, prettiness in poor taste, and false beauty, all that was ersatz in art at the end of the last century and the beginning of ours. Clever dealers understood that true ugliness would be successful with those who were sick and tired of false beauty. Those same dealers understood how much the intellectuals would need a good pretext to demonstrate their intellectualism, and that those intellectuals would defend, encourage, and maintain all that might furnish them with such a possibility.

"And so, two phenomena made their appearance in the modern life of art: art dealers, who until then had held but modest roles, and art critics, who previously did not exist at all. Sainte-Beuve, Diderot, Baudelaire, and more recently Guillaume Apollinaire have been isolated cases. These were poets and writers who introduced into their practice writing on painting, mostly intended for their friends; they were not art critics. On the contrary, apart from some very rare exceptions, the art critic, born with modern art, is a writer who, unable to write a good book, finds it easier to critique and give advice to his contemporaries.

"Unacknowledged geniuses thus found a way to be read and listened to. It is they who have contributed to the anarchy and confusion that already for almost half a century have reigned in the brains of lovers of art. Show me the serious and responsible man who desires to claim *the role of the art critic*?...

"Of a masterpiece one can say only that it is a masterpiece, the rest is the secret of the painter who made it. Everything else said about a masterpiece is nothing more than literature and useless chatter that cannot explain anything better than we can see it with our own eyes.

"With a few words one can describe the qualities and defects of a good but not excellent painting, on the condition, you understand, that one is a true connoisseur of painting or, better yet, a talented painter. Of a completely horrible painting, like almost all paintings made today, one can say everything in a single sentence: that is, that it would have been better had the painting never been made. Everything that might be of some use to art or those concerned with it would thus be said.

"But, dear Maestro, I think that instead of talking about that which should be said and written, I should rather talk of how much has been said and written.

"I must first of all point out, and you have moreover already noticed on your own, that art critics have invented a whole modern phraseology and have managed to see in some current paintings—in which there is absolutely nothing to see—things so extraordinary that they would have frightened the old masters, had they been able to read them. Certainly, those old masters would never have imagined that paintings could be so complicated to look at; they believed only that they were difficult to make.

"The intellectuals saw in the art critic's obscure and hermetic discourses the ideal means for intellectualism to triumph over true and concrete intelligence.

"Thus was initiated intellectualism's frenetic race against its hidden but implacable destiny, which consists in the arrival of total stupidity, the solitary reason for its existence.

"Intellectualism is directly tied to *snobbism*, which is also a new and negative phenomenon in the milieu of modern art.

"The origin of the word *snobbism* is *sine nobilitate*, without nobility. In England, when young men of the people began to attend the universities, in order to distinguish them from the other students of aristocratic origins, the abbreviation *snob*, short for *sine nobilitate*, would be written beside their names and surnames in the university registers. Those students, who were the children of rich but simple people, didn't have impeccable upbringings and in fact displayed those ridiculous behaviors that are a characteristic of the nouveau riche. As such, the aristocrats gave them that short and unequivocal name, *snobs*. And it is that very word that modern intellectuals went seeking to indicate their larger refinement.

"The sages say that truth always shines through and ultimately triumphs; perhaps it is such truth that inspired the *snobs* to give themselves such a merited title.

"Writing their articles, almost all art critics concern themselves with no more than a single thing: demonstrating their skill and intelligence to the world.

"In their writings they have found a way to relate elucubrations so obscure that they themselves have ended up no longer comprehending anything. From those sentences completely devoid of communal sense have been born aspects of modern literature and also the manner of expressing oneself and even of thinking (if, that is, one can speak here of thinking) in intellectual environments.

"When one witnesses gatherings in literary salons—and it makes no difference if these gatherings take place in old Europe or in the New World—the conversations, the discussions, the opinions are always the same. If a person travels frequently, he has the impression he is dreaming because, for example, in New York he hears the same sentences regarding painting or literature that one or two weeks before he heard in Paris or another European capital.

"The worldwide uniformity of *snobs* has lent them the appearance of talking automatons rather than living beings. A living person, no matter how simple, has a brain that functions, even if in a rudimentary way; that is absolutely not the case with *snobs*."

Isabella Far fell silent, and Mr. Dudron, becoming animated, expressed in enthusiastic terms all his admiration for the exactness of her observations and for the clarity with which she formulated them. Always eager to be educated, he entreated her to go on. "I would also like to know, madam," he said, "how one can explain the great number—the mass—of intellectuals in modern life when once there were no more than small groups of people, truly superior, who were concerned with and interested in elevated matters of the spirit, and it was these people who were called the intellectuals?"

Isabella Far, who had listened with great attention to Mr. Dudron's question, reflected for a moment and then said, "Listen, Maestro, I think that this is possible to explain in the following way: today's intellectual is a special phenomenon who has absolutely nothing to do with the intellectual of the past. This intellectual isn't just a product of social progress but is above all a product of global economic evolution. At first when nobles lost the exclusive privilege of wealth, the common folk who had achieved material well-being didn't worry about anything but the external aspects of their lives. This is very logical if one remembers that for too many generations those who rose from the lower classes had admired and envied the brilliant and elegant lives led by nobles and other eminent persons.

"The nouveau riche, whose training was no more than elementary, saw only the superficial side of noble life—that is to say the luxury, the comfort, the entertainment—and all that became their ideal. The nouveau riche believed, and wrongly, that the superiority of the nobles over others consisted solely in the luxury, the entertainment, that is, in the superficial parts of their lives. The new classes, formed from those who rose from the masses, tried to prove their superiority by putting on luxurious clothing, having horses and vehicles—in short, through an elegant and enviable lifestyle.

"Little by little these new classes of merchants and, later, manufacturers, began to educate themselves because their business activities required a certain level of education. They even created a social life, seeking to make it similar to that of the noble classes. Still, their efforts remained concentrated on elegance and external things. The rapid development of commerce and manufacturing spread more and more material well-being to an ever-increasing number of individuals. It became common for ordinary people to lead lives at a very high level. As a result, once more huge fortunes and an exceptional effort became necessary to impress others. But individuals in possession of truly huge fortunes were rare, while the number of those who felt the need to seem superior to their peers grew continually. At this point men remembered those spiritual qualities by which one might eventually impose upon others and rise up in their eyes. And so our passion for intelligence began around the end of the last century and has continued to develop—not as a superior quality of the human spirit, but as a useful means for pretentious and ultimately stupid men to seem exceptional. Here, Maestro, is the origin of modern intellectualism."

Isabella Far fell silent. Mr. Dudron thanked her warmly for the precious enlightenments that she had furnished and congratulated her even more profoundly on her astonishing gifts of philosophical intelligence, observational spirit, critique, extraordinary logic, and clarity.

It was beginning to get dark, and the air was growing humid. Gallantly offering his arm to Isabella Far, Mr. Dudron accompanied her to her house, paying her every kind of compliment, even for her name. "You see, madam," he said, "your name has something oracular, something prophetic about it. In French it sounds like the word *phare*, the light that reveals the port to seafarers; in English, on the other hand, it means *far*, and indeed you do go very far with your thoughts, very far, but always with that overpowering logic that is the prerogative of superior spirits."

After having escorted Isabella Far, Mr. Dudron set out to return to his own home. He was about to start toward his residence when he ran into a sculptor friend, a very serious artist who had achieved an absolutely first-rate status with his tireless work. This friend had just one obsession, or rather, a weakness: billiards. But it wasn't his passion for the game that constituted his weakness as much as the relentlessness with which he sought to pass for a maestro, a virtuoso of the game, while he was no more than a mediocre player. Mr. Dudron teased him for this, and running into him that evening, he resumed his ridiculing, concluding, "My dear friend, your case reminds me of that of another friend of mine who left our city some years ago to settle abroad. He was, like you, a serious artist, full of talent, and one of those men, rare today, who understands painting. Nevertheless he based all his self-esteem in the culinary arts. He boasted about knowing how to cook and proudly claimed that he had a particular talent for preparing a plate of spaghetti and for making mayonnaise. If he erred in making his spaghetti or his mayonnaise he was seized by such a hysterical crisis, such a fit of rage and desperation that whatever he might have felt bungling a painting after months of work would have been a child's joke in comparison. If you have time to take a little walk with me I will recount to you two episodes concerning this gentleman."

Enticed by the promise of hearing Mr. Dudron tell stories, the sculptor immediately agreed to accompany him to his door—he knew that Mr. Dudron's tales were always entertaining and that he had great talent as a humorist and storyteller. They set out, one beside the other, at a slow and measured pace, and at a certain point Mr. Dudron began: "A few months before his departure I ran into my friend at an art dealer's gallery, and he said to me, 'If you don't have other plans tomorrow, my wife and I will come to your house and I will make you a plate of spaghetti—you know it is my specialty. Don't prepare anything else because once you have eaten a plate of spaghetti as I make it, you will be full for at least two days.' The next day, much earlier than the hour we had agreed upon, he came to my house with his wife. I had taken care that he would find on my kitchen table two packages of the highest quality spaghetti as well as grated cheese and butter.

"My friend began by taking off his jacket and rolling up the sleeves of his shirt. Then, he asked for a pot. I pointed to the one I used to cook spaghetti, but my friend, smiling sardonically, said to me, 'It isn't possible to make anything good in a pot like that. The most important factor for the success of a plate of spaghetti is the pot's capacity; the strands of spaghetti must be boiled in a great volume of water so that they don't stick to one another and make a soft and homogenous block. As they are boiled the spaghetti must be able to swim freely like fish in an aquarium. Each strand must be able to voyage on its own during the cooking—rising to the surface, sinking down, reaching the bottom, circulating between the water's layers, in short, moving with full freedom without risking getting attached to the other strands, its brothers—and that is why it is necessary to have a vessel with great capacity.'

"After speaking these words and without even waiting for me to reply, my friend set about looking for another vessel. He settled on an enormous metal bucket whose purpose among the other kitchen implements was not clear. A horrible suspicion arose in my mind—that that bucket had previously served to boil dirty linens—however, I remained silent and tried to think of other things. My friend took possession of the bucket and filled it with water until it was overflowing. Then, with horrible grimaces and extreme effort—because the bucket took on considerable weight when completely full—he placed it on the burner at the risk of shattering the stove. Waiting, the hours passed. With his watch in hand and his eyes fixed on the surface of the water, my friend looked like a scientist, an inventor, one of those heroes of science whose portraits you might see in the second part of the *Nuovissimo Melzi* unabridged dictionary in the act of following the evolution of an experiment of capital importance, of monitoring the success of an invention destined to completely revolutionize human life.

"But the water continued to not-boil. The grandfather clock in the dining room sounded nine fifteen. I thought with some concern about how I generally dined at eight. My friend's face shrank slightly, but he managed to control himself and stiffened into a severe and obstinate posture. To interrupt the tragic atmosphere caused by the wait, he took a large package of salt that he found in a kitchen cabinet, and I saw him throw a pinch so tiny into the water that it would have been barely enough to salt the contents of a shot glass. With much tact and prudence I gestured to him. 'No,' my friend responded in the tone of a great perfectionist who is secure in what he does and won't take criticism from the ignorant. 'No,' he repeated, 'it is a great error to believe that salt enhances the flavor of food. It is absolutely false that food that is salty is more flavorful than it would be with little or even no salt at all.' Then he added, approaching me with a quieter voice as if he wanted to confide a secret of extreme importance, 'One must leave foods to their normal and natural flavor; in this consists the beginning of great cooking.'

"The clock sounded ten o'clock. Finally, around ten thirty, the water began to boil. My friend flew to throw in the spaghetti, which had the effect of immediately arresting the boiling. Later the water started to boil again, but at a slower rate. Then my friend took up another task: armed with a fork, he periodically seized a strand of spaghetti, pulled it from the boiling water, then put it in his mouth and ruminated slowly, staring in front of him with an absent air like an enologist who is about to taste the wines of a very important winery. Other times he would take a strand between his thumb and pointer finger and squeeze it with slow and gradual precision, then he would release his fingers with a rapid movement to examine the pasta's level of doneness. Finally, after several other complicated operations, he announced with a solemn tone that the spaghetti was cooked and we could come to the table. The grandfather clock in the dining room sounded eleven o'clock. My friend's wife, unable to resist the wringing of her stomach, had already eaten almost all the cheese in the cupboard.

"We sat at the table. The bowl of spaghetti steamed and formed a magnificent block, compact and uniform. With a spoon and fork I tried to detach a piece to serve to my friend's wife, but seeing my great effort my friend became pale—his hands began to tremble and the muscles in his face shrank into an indescribable expression of rage, spite, and distress. It was a true disaster! The block of spaghetti was so dense that I needed some time to break a piece off. Moreover, the grated cheese had coagulated in some spots while others were absolutely naked. The insipidness of that boiled whitish mass surpassed all that can be imagined. My friend suffered the torments of hell. The recognition of this outcome after all the precautions he had taken, after all the theories he had espoused, prostrated him with an immense shame, an infinite humiliation. I believe that in that moment he wished he could be very far away, deep in the bowels of the earth. I believe that in that moment he wished for the immense distances of the African deserts to open between me and him, for there to appear limitless oceans, chains of insurmountable mountains, and then forests and more forests, impenetrable forests!

"My friend's wife barely tasted her spaghetti. Out of delicacy I tried to eat, and tried, too, to console my friend, telling him that if the spaghetti wasn't a total success it was probably because of the water. I told him that there are regions where the water is particularly suited to a successful plate of spaghetti, even augments its nutritional qualities. But my friend wasn't listening to me at all.

"Knocked flat by the catastrophe, he couldn't utter a word and his chin trembled as though he was suffering from malarial fever. Finally, with the pretense of being very tired and needing to wake up early the next morning, he said good night and left, pushing his wife in front of him and stepping rigidly with the gait of a sleepwalker, like that character in the Old Testament whom God commanded to walk without turning around."

The sculptor, who had not stopped snorting with laughter during the entire story of the spaghetti, congratulated Mr. Dudron on the great comedy of his tale and on his truly exceptional talents as a narrator. But he reminded him that he had promised two stories and the sculptor wouldn't leave before he had been told the second. Mr. Dudron gratified him and began like this: "The second story is also about my painter friend. This one is shorter than the last but even more dramatic; this time it is about the preparation of *mayonnaise*. Here's what happened. A few months after the spaghetti story, my friend rented an old dilapidated villa in the countryside for the summer. One day he invited me to dine. It was July and the heat was canicular. 'I will make you mayonnaise,' he told me. 'You know that one of my specialties is making an excellent mayonnaise, reaching the rare degree of perfection that is the total success of that classic sauce, a degree of perfection that few great cooks have achieved. It is a truly difficult undertaking of which I have become a master. I won't say any more. Come to dine in the evening the day after tomorrow and you will learn something about my mayonnaise!'

"On the day and hour appointed for dinner I was at my friend's. The old dilapidated villa he had rented was in an arid countryside; the heat was suffocating. Not far from there was a large industrial building where they turned the excrement of men or animals into fertilizer for the cultivation of the earth. Every now and then the hot wind blowing from the south carried whiffs of its intolerable stench. I found my friend settled at a table on a kind of veranda below the feeble light of an acetylene gas lamp that also gave off an odor that was anything but pleasing. On the table were bowls, saucers, plates, bottles, and eggs. My friend received me with the busy air of a man who has no time to lose: 'I am getting ready to make the mayonnaise,' he said. 'It is an extremely delicate operation, but you will see what a masterpiece I will achieve!'

"I approached the table with the presentiment of a catastrophe. My friend cracked the eggs into a bowl and began to drizzle small quantities of olive oil on them, mixing with a fork: 'It's the principle of emulsion,' he declared, beating the eggs with his fork. 'As you know, in painting emulsions are a medium that provides paints with oiliness, preciousness, fluidity—the fascination and mystery the old masters recognized and today's painters have lost even the memory of. *In emulsion veritas!*' But I realized that his expression was becoming apprehensive while he stared at the nascent mayonnaise. For a moment he paused in his constant stirring of the mixture, leaned down to take a closer look, and then began to beat the whole of it with his fork, but with distress looming on his face. I, too, moved nearer to look and saw in the bowl a kind of yellow liquid scattered with distinct pieces that seemed coagulated—tiny icebergs in a saffron-colored sea. My friend suspended his operation. 'It's no use,' he said in a voice rendered hoarse by emotion, 'I must start over. It is the heat that has dealt me this ugly hand. Naturally cold climates and seasons aid this kind of operation. But you'll see that I will succeed. In life one must never despair, and we artists must always be the first to model will, patience, constancy, and courage.'

"Having delivered this small lecture, he took another bowl, called the housekeeper, and asked her to bring him more oil, of a superior quality to the one he had been using. The housekeeper brought him another bottle of oil, and he recommenced the operation while saying, as though to himself, 'The quality of the oil is very important. Extremely important. One cannot insist enough on the importance of the oil in the success of the mayonnaise!'

"As he spoke, I saw that his face was starting once more to shrivel. I looked in the bowl: the sauce was in full decomposition. Large pieces of coagulated liquid leaped beneath the blows of the fork. I saw my friend whiten frighteningly and with a kind of death rattle place the fork on the table and lower his head to his chest; it was a tired and resigned gesture, the gesture of an athlete *giving up*. But he collected himself immediately and exclaimed, 'I understand! How did I not think of this before! It's the eggs! It's definitely the eggs! With this dog-day heat one needs the freshest eggs. Svetonia! Svetonia!' (this was the housekeeper's name), 'go and find me today's eggs, ideally laid this afternoon!'

"The housekeeper rushed into the courtyard; we heard the squawk and chatter of birds disturbed in their sleep. The housekeeper returned a short time later with eggs covered in dirt, straw encrusted in their filth. My friend set once more to work. This time he worked more slowly; his movements had something solemn about them. It felt like this was the definitive turn. The scene acquired the magnitude of a Greek tragedy. Laboring, my friend spoke as if in a dream, with his eyes fixed on the bowl: 'It was the eggs! It was the eggs, which weren't fresh enough!' I discerned on his face the progress of the operation. Suddenly I saw that he was beginning to tremble all over his body. I looked into the bowl: larger than ever the icebergs had reappeared. My friend paused his operation. Right at that moment some large night-flyers burned themselves in the acetylene gas lamp and fell into the decomposed mayonnaise, writhing like wild ducks would in the water of a pond if shot by a hunter. It was the absolute limit! I heard a smothered sob and my friend, foaming at the mouth, crashed to the floor of the veranda. Fortunately, a straw chair behind him prevented his head from crashing directly on the stone. The housekeeper, who had witnessed the scene, let out a shout that caused my friend's wife to rush out of the living room. Together, all three of us flew to lay him upon a bed. He had completely lost consciousness. A doctor called in a hurry attended to him. He came to forty-five minutes later. The doctor remained for some time after my friend had regained his senses and advised him to stop cooking or else the severity of his attacks would continue to increase and he could not completely discount the risk of a fatal outcome."

The sculptor writhed with laughter. Meanwhile, they had arrived at Mr. Dudron's door. His friend wished him a good night and thanked him warmly for the stories of the spaghetti and the mayonnaise.

"Ah, yes," thought Mr. Dudron, entering his apartment, "there are people who put all their self-worth into the little things, the insignificant facts of life. I too am not entirely happy when someone says I have the air of a sweet man, inoffensive and sentimental, and would prefer they said I have the face of a rabble-rouser or of a Western bandit; but in spite of that, the disappointment I feel doesn't reach the point of making me fall suddenly into a hysterical crisis. What the hell, everything has its limit! These are sad things, I know—alas, very sad! Something senseless, foolish, insane, and illogical emanates from all of this, and even though it can all be explained with clarity from a psychological point of view, it is impossible not to feel profoundly discouraged. Why are people who appear the same so different at the core? It is fate, always fate, eternal fate with which one tries to explain everything."

Articulating to himself this opinion on fate, Mr. Dudron went on to think that perhaps it was also fate that had brought him one summer morning, very early, to one of the most astonishing displays he had ever seen in his life, rich in adventure and spectacle. Mr. Dudron remembered. That morning insomnia had driven him from bed much earlier than dawn. He remembered that getting up, he had had a vague impression that the ancient Romans, in the time of the republic and even in the time of the empire, must have felt something, perceived certain odors like those that he, Mr. Dudron, sensed in that moment.

It was a clear, hot morning in late summer. He had left the city and reached the edge of a forest. The sun, just over the horizon, sent off its oblique rays, which filtered through the tree trunks: golden phantoms, like little nets in outline (similar to hexahedrons), went from tree to tree. Further on there was a light mist. Winged insects remained motionless at some distance from the sun like minuscule helicopters. No sounds, no birdsong.

In front of Mr. Dudron there was a large cage mounted on four wheels. Three lions, awake and seated, were locked in; they looked out. They had been brought there for the fair that was soon to begin; this cage had arrived before the others. All around, dismantled stalls lay on the ground. The manager wasn't there—no doubt he had gone to city hall or to the police for permits. The lions were alone. The shutters had been removed to allow air into the cage, and the bars of their prison were visible. All three were leaning against the back of the cage as if it held all their safety. The largest, probably the oldest, shook his heavy head, wrinkling his severe face and staring fixedly at a point in the forest before him, a point below the trees that was lost in shadow....

For all that a suburban lion can know of existence, this one must have imagined the mysterious forest as a malicious place where the blows of the whip and lash landed endlessly from each branch. Perhaps the old lion wondered if the wicked species of two-legged tamers swarmed from these parts in a savage state, always ready to trap him in jaws even he would not have wanted to encounter at dusk in a deserted place....

To the right of the cage, above a rise in the landscape, a convent for orphans extended its great aviary facade. Even during holidays it held closed within its walls young girls without parents or friends.

Mr. Dudron remembered. An undefinable melancholy rippled in the air. There was a gray sensation, something strangely neutral that rose with the mist and spread in the silence and in the summer morning light. A strange atmosphere in that still deserted place where, in that moment, the only prisoners breathing were virgins and lions.

Recalling that memory, Mr. Dudron remained lost in his thoughts. Then, mechanically, he went about preparing his bed, placing on his night table the indispensable glass of water, box of matches, candle, and watch. Finally, he undressed and lay down.

He was a bit tired; he had had a rather eventful day, and now he felt great pleasure in stretching out voluptuously in his bed. On an easel, as was his wont, he kept propped the last painting he had worked on, which depicted a man with a proud and barbarous look, enveloped to his chin in a big black cape, sitting on a small horse with a long mane and muscular body.

Around the rider there was a wild landscape of rocks and dark fir trees. Mr. Dudron had already titled this unfinished painting: he called it *Hannibal*. Now, stretched out in his bed, he looked at it while he smoked his pipe and lost himself in reveries. Meanwhile, over his thoughts and the images he saw so beautifully, there descended the cloud of a good sleep, the vapors of sweet sleep, of sweet sleep restoring the toils and thoughts of mortals… Hannibal!… that was the name of the barber's assistant whom Mr. Dudron had for some months been teaching, with patience worthy of an ancient pedagogue, to cut his hair as he wanted it—that is to say, not too short, with the part on one side and a lock over his forehead and, above all, without asking him at the end if he wanted a massage. It was not easy to educate a barber's assistant in this respect. It is incredible how long it takes to make a barber understand that he does not need to cut your hair so short and that, after having cut it, he does not have to ask you if you want a massage, with lotions for your scalp or anything else.… Sometimes it happened that after having spent a year habituating a barber to the manner in which he wanted his hair cut, he, Mr. Dudron, was obliged to go, to leave the city, to move, and then he had to start all over again with another barber in the new place. It was all too much!

Mr. Dudron was in the habit of going to the hairdresser on Tuesdays in the early afternoon. Because there weren't usually customers around at that hour he could be sure of being seen immediately. At that hour the young man did not have anyone to take care of and would sit, yawning, smoking, and reading the newspaper. When Mr. Dudron appeared, the young man, named Hannibal, would get up and invite him to sit in the barber's chair. This reminded Mr. Dudron of another scene: he had the habit, with certain houses he frequented, of going, as with the barber, during the early afternoon and on a day of the week when he knew there would be few clients. There, too, when he appeared in the parlor doorway, the girl with whom he was in the habit of *retiring* would get up and walk before him, climbing and yawning, to the second floor. The similarity between these two scenes had ended up creating in the sensitive and impressionable soul of Mr. Dudron a confused and complicated feeling; he had ended up seeing Hannibal, the young hairdresser, in a strange light, he had ended up seeing him *otherwise*; while Hannibal, with his hand on the clippers, labored *interminably* on his neck hair, Mr. Dudron felt a vague discomfort, a strange apprehension and at the same time a certain shame; it seemed to him that at any moment Hannibal would place the clippers on the marble counter, walk up the stairs, and that he, Mr. Dudron, would follow him....

The vapors of sleep rose and rose without respite in Mr. Dudron's mind. The images became confused; only a name, Hannibal, resounded clearly in his memory. Hannibal! Before the strange world of dreams, the great, thick curtain of reality and logic opened slowly. Mr. Dudron had closed his eyes, but other eyes had opened in him, and it was with great surprise and curiosity that he *watched* the spectacle that unfolded before him. The painting had disappeared, and the walls of his room and everything that he was used to seeing around him while lying down had also disappeared. A long chain of men and horses, bowed under the weight of their baggage, advanced laboriously along the steep trails of a wild alpine setting.

Every once in a while the drawn-out trumpeting of elephants resounded in the dark valleys, awakening in the solemn alpine silence the echoes of the mountain. A leader, a general, hair tossed by the wind, clenched between his legs the thin flanks of a small, black, muscular horse. Sometimes he advanced with the front line and other times he paused to encourage the tired and desperate soldiers sitting on the stones littering the path. Still other times this leader scrutinized those white peaks from the top of a rock; he studied them intensely, as if he wished to interrogate them—those solitary peaks, those heights covered with snow, crowned with clouds, motionless and majestic, like gigantic gods.

Night arrived, a deep night, and the fire from the bivouacs tinted the darkness red. With a pensive air the general listened to the nostalgic songs, the sad melopoeia of the young mercenaries hastily recruited from the wilds of the Iberian Peninsula.

When the songs' lament went silent, he could hear climbing up to him the whistle of the wind that raged in the ravines and the mysterious whispering of the great spruce forests and the sonorous murmuring of the rapids that gushed from the dark gorges with icy moisture....

When Mr. Dudron woke it was late: around eleven. He was sorry to have slept so long despite the suggestive dream he had had. "Anyhow," Mr. Dudron said to himself, "you can't live on dreams, goddammit. You must also think about reality."

The town clock struck eleven thirty.

Suddenly Mr. Dudron remembered there was barely time to throw on his clothes and jump on a bus to a small church outside the city to attend a requiem mass for a student from the School of Fine Arts, where Mr. Dudron had taught a drawing course.

When the student was still alive, his classmates would make fun of him, calling him Mr. Mellone after that strong-smelling gourd he loved to treat himself to during the hot summer months. This youngster, whose financial situation was extremely modest, had expired in a hospital for the poor after a maltreated bout of typhoid fever. The nickname Mr. Mellone had always irritated him terribly, and Mr. Dudron remembered how this youth had once lost his head completely because a classmate who was half hidden behind a corner in the corridor of the school kept calling him Mr. Mellone, provoking general hilarity among the students. He had then pulled a razor from his pocket and, with bulging eyes and his face set in a grimace, had thrown himself at his classmate. Who knows what would have happened if the student attacked so suddenly hadn't thought to flee, running around the plaster casts on wooden bases that lined the school corridor. Below the immovable gazes and distant, smiling expressions of various Joves, Junos, and Hercules, he had managed to evade his aggressor and take shelter in the anatomy classroom behind the double-locked door.

The memory of all of these spiteful acts to which they had subjected him when he was still alive drove the academy's students, consumed with tardy remorse, to hold a mass for the repose of the soul of their deceased classmate. The mass was to be held outside the city in a small church in the countryside situated amid olive trees.

When Mr. Dudron arrived, the mass was almost over. It was a beautiful winter morning, clear and cold. It had snowed the evening before, and the ground was still completely white.

Immaculate patches like tufts of cotton wool remained attached to the trunks and branches of the olive trees, some of which had been struck by lightning and had contorted, burned, and split trunks that brought to mind the damned souls in Dante's inferno. Those trees, so evocative of the southern countryside, contrasted with the Nordic effect of the field all white with snow and the background of dark, low, gray clouds against which pairs of crows flew, heavily emitting every once in a while those caws Mr. Dudron had always loved. At the close of mass, the students emerged from the church rubbing their hands, which were red from the cold, and raising the collars of their overcoats. As it was already well past noon, they entered a small inn. They dined on bitter herbs, duly washed and dressed with oil, salt, and lemon; they had olives and black bread, then a cup of black coffee, flavored with anise, in which they dunked dry biscuits. This meal, though light, warmed them and dispelled a bit the sadness brought on by the mass in that small, remote church in the snow-covered countryside and by the memory of their departed classmate, whom they had made something of a victim of their youthful thoughtlessness. A guitar appeared and, passed from person to person, ended up in the hands of a pupil who knew how to play and who began to strum rhythmic chords. He struck up the chorus of a nostalgic love song, and everyone went outside singing with the guitarist in the lead. Their feet sank into the snow, and every now and then they heard the cawing of the crows. Under the low gray sky, the sad love song's refrain got lost with the guitar's harmonies in the cold and tranquil air.

The streets are white with snow
Yet see—I'm always here!
Oh, my girl, take care of our love
For it's a bad world!

With his hat pulled down over his head, his coat thrown over his shoulders, and his hands in his pockets, Mr. Dudron walked alongside the group of singers. He walked looking at the ground with a pensive air; he had the classic look of the democratically minded intellectual; he conjured his life, the years that had flown by, and he felt that vague nostalgia for the past that sometimes pricked him. He saw himself alone in that colorful city, pursuing a fleeting ideal; then he saw himself even longer ago in that other city, white and solemn, in whose southern gardens, beneath the clear sky of those beautiful winter afternoons, oranges and mandarins shone in all their splendor, ardent colors silhouetted against the dark green of the leaves like so many little Venetian lanterns hanging from the branches....

The song's refrain spread...

Our torments are their joy
Our tears are our treasure...

Mr. Dudron continued to walk alongside the group of singers as a corporal leads recruits through a drill.

They had arrived at the gates of the city. Twilight had fallen; a long red brightening on the horizon augured that the next day would be beautiful. Mr. Dudron remembered a proverb from his region: red sky at night, sailor's delight. This made him vaguely melancholy, as he had an extremely sensitive soul and dreaded clear and sunny days.

"When the sun shines and the sky is clear," thought Mr. Dudron, "our misfortunes seem more profound. Upon the invisible staircase erected in the unfathomable blue, we climb as on a taut ladder toward a hanging trapeze, and from there we throw our glances out over the world and over life, which we should rightly call *our world* and *our life*. On that ineffable swing we launch ourselves into the void, and with every thrust the void grabs us by the stomach and vertigo contracts our senses; always higher, forward and back, and always farther, forward and back. Past years and future years, they are nothing but folly—the measure of time! But when, during my sleepless hours, I listen toward the end of the night to the heavy sanitation carts stopping in front of houses to carry the garbage away, then, sometimes, among those sounds, I hear something like the distant echo of eternity. Chastity of my interior life! And you, faithful housekeepers, you who were my first teachers, who first gave me my taste for art, for beautiful painting, for love and tobacco, may God bless you! I can never repay what you have given me. If I could, to express my gratitude, I'd bring you to the theater on a Sunday afternoon so you could see onstage the devil in a black sweater who shoots in a room and then opens the window and hurls himself into the void like a diver into water. And after the show I'd take you to a pastry shop for a cup of chocolate with whipped cream and hot *brioches*. If I can never do all of this, don't be offended! Don't be offended since in this sad impossibility you'd see the debt I had to pay destiny for the purest joys I enjoyed in your company and the new horizons that have since then opened to my astonished eyes—the eyes of a thinker and poet!"

When they arrived at the main city gate, Mr. Dudron took his leave of the students and returned home. Many thoughts tormented him, all having to do with painting. The mystery of discovering its origins. He searched in his notebooks. He leafed through the books he owned that dealt with this subject, which is so mysterious that art critics today are careful about broaching it. One of these books attracted his attention, as happened every time he rifled through these works. The title of the book was *The Art of Painting in Oil* and then, in smaller letters: *Being a History of the Various Processes and Materials Employed, from Its Discovery, by Hubert and John Van Eyck, to the Present Time.*

The author was named J. F. L. Mérimée, but he had absolutely nothing in common with the author of *Carmen*. He had been the permanent secretary of the Royal School of Fine Arts, and what he wrote was certainly more useful to Mr. Dudron than the works of the homonymous Prosper Mérimée. J. F. L. Mérimée's book was printed in Paris in 1830 by Madame Huzard (née Vallat-la-Chapelle). As a preface to the book there appeared an excerpt from the report made to the Academy of Fine Arts of the Royal Academy of France by M. Quatremère de Quincy. This excerpt was written in a clear style, full of logic, and was consequently the precise opposite of the pretentious, incomprehensible articles, completely lacking in utility or interest, that art critics and intellectuals today dedicate to modern painting and to painting in general. Here, for example, are a few sentences from the preface: "The precepts which the author has collected, extended, and developed... are not so much intended to teach this art, as to lay before the artist the proper materials for painting... A principal object has been to collect and carefully describe the numerous processes used in oil painting from its earliest appearance to our own time. The result of this investigation shows that the older masters of the Venetian and Flemish schools, did not paint as moderns do, with pure oils, but that they tempered their colours with varnishes; to which must be attributed the state of preservation in which we find their pictures."

Mr. Dudron remained profoundly interested in different passages of this book, which he had been reading and rereading already for many years. He lingered once more on a few pages that made him meditate at length every time. Speaking of the days when Jan van Eyck worked in Flanders, J. F. L. Mérimée wrote:

"At that period the artists all painted in distemper... and they afterwards coated their pictures with varnish, which communicated a transparency and brightness to the colours, defending them, at the same time, against the injurious actions of the atmosphere. The idea of mixing the colours, in the first instance, with varnish, is sufficiently obvious, not to have suggested itself to the human mind; and it is not unlikely that some artists had already attempted to make it available; but many difficulties were to be surmounted ere a novel method could be fairly substituted for that of distemper, to which they were habituated; the artists, in fact, not having the requisite information or knowledge of the means by which their efforts might have been successful. The varnish in use at that period was of an oily and very viscous nature; nor did the practitioners know how to render it sufficiently fluid to mix well with the colours, and thereby render them equally manageable as they are in distemper....

"Thus, as I have already observed, the idea of incorporating the varnish with the colour, being the most simple, we may infer that it would naturally, in the first instance, occur to the mind of Van Eyck. The object of his researches would have been but imperfectly fulfilled if his colours had been prepared as ours, and, equally liable to dry in, had required the aid of a coat of varnish to draw out their clearness and brilliancy.... In the pictures of Van Eyck, as well as those of the painters who followed his method, the colours have not been used simply with oil of a more or less drying quality, but that they were mixed with varnish; which is the cause of the surprising preservation we witness in so many of the oldest pictures, and which have retained their brilliancy of tone much better than the greater part of those which were painted in the last century."

Mr. Dudron paused in his reading and reflected, "It's incredible," he thought, "how this is all completely foreign to today's painters; their interest in their art—that passion, joy, and emotion that once animated painters and, notwithstanding the difficulties and vicissitudes of life, made them happy—has completely disappeared. This explains the boredom that torments today's painters; the art they make ultimately doesn't interest them—it doesn't amuse them at all. *Surprise* has abandoned their studies.

The very surprise that in the past, in the days of good and beautiful painting, when each artist sought to paint better than all the others, when each artist worked daily to take a step forward and therefore sought—like a magician, like an alchemist, with passion—the means that would allow him to realize that progress; the very surprise that was beside them, invisible and present, so that sometimes, when they turned to look at a painting they had finished, or when they returned to their studio after having been away even for just a moment, they might exclaim, '*I* made that!'—that surprise, I say, no longer exists."

For a moment Mr. Dudron considered starting to paint, but the problems of painting and the causes of its terrifying decadence continued to assail his spirit. He placed a bookmark in Mérimée's book, grabbed his coat and hat, and prepared to leave his studio. As he descended the stairs to the street he thought, "I must see Isabella Far again; she is the only person who can tell me something truly intelligent about this subject, something right and logical. It is almost noon. At this hour she leaves the library or goes to consult the records at the School of Fine Arts—records compiled in the eighteenth century, when the school was called the Royal Academy of Painting. There, for hours at a time, she reads the memos of conferences held by Largillière, Oudry, and other teachers who worked in that magnificent century that, unlike our own, was full of artists of genius and during which talent could be found on every street corner."

He followed the avenue lined with pepper trees because he knew that the great thinker took this road on her way home.

He had been walking for several minutes when he realized that Isabella Far was coming toward him from afar. He approached her, greeted her, asked after her health, and added quickly that he greatly needed her to clarify certain questions about painting and its current decadence. Very kindly, Isabella Far accepted. "I will gladly explain that which you ask," she responded. "Accompany me to my house, and we will talk as we walk. Now, dear Maestro, tell me in a few words what it is that you wish to know."

Mr. Dudron reflected for a moment and then said, "I would like to know further, madame, how you explain the existence of art critics and the figure of the modern collector, and, in general, I want you to tell me more about what you think of modern art."

"Very well, Maestro," answered Isabella Far. "Right from the start art dealers made use in their commercial activity of art critics and intellectuals for the sole aim of earning money for themselves; artists without talent used them to earn recognition.

"The *snobs*, who didn't have serious preparation, who lacked artistic comprehension and true intelligence, were guided and exploited by the dealers, critics, and artists, as all of these people, unable to root their activities in real value, were driven to ground them in the stupidity of others.

"The entire *bluff* rested on so-called *invented painting* and 'stylized' art. The value of these paintings was not dependent on the esteemed values that had guided painters through the middle of the nineteenth century, the era around which decadence began. That is to say: quality, design, the preciousness of the materials, the delicacy of the models, the mastery of execution; all told, the painterly quality of the work. On the contrary, the value of *invented painting* was based on intellectual invention, the expression of abstract ideas, surreal eccentricities, and idiosyncrasies very close to dementia, infantilism, occultism, and so on… in short, the value of this new painting consisted in the precise opposite of all that constitutes great painting, which is concrete, positive, and utterly realized.

"At this point, to avoid misunderstanding, we must clarify that the true value of an invented work is found in the revelation that led the painter to make it. After all, it is still debatable whether a revelation—which in the case of painting is an incomplete fact—can be sufficient to make of a painting a great work of art. A painting masterpiece must contain not only the elements of idea and subject but, above all, the *inspiration* of the execution and material. We can't say if the *idea* is more important in music and philosophy than it is in painting, but I would suggest that in music and philosophy she is more self-sufficient and has less need for accessories.

"A painting made following a revelation certainly has value, but it is a relative value, while a painting masterpiece, that is to say pure and complete art, has an *absolute* value.

"When one analyzes the causes of modern painting's divulgation, one cannot conclude that they reside in the phenomenon of revelation found in certain modern works. In the mass of canvases that pass for extraordinary, those in which one can find a *revelation* are very rare. In the others, where this phenomenon is lacking, one sees but a terrible effort to replace the nonexistent revelation with the quest for originality and ideas. In these paintings, random objects and lines are put together without any spiritual or artistic rationale. There is no revelation in these paintings, only great stupidity, an absolute void, and the complete absence of talent.

"Naturally one cannot expect that the lovers of modern painting can actually see revelation in a canvas. Revelation is a phenomenon that is difficult to see or comprehend for a person whose comprehension, intelligence, and feeling for art are not the high comprehension, intelligence, and feeling of a real connoisseur.

"The amateur, the modern collector, doesn't even perceive the poor quality, the poor execution that is so evident in these paintings lacking in revelation. People today are so accustomed to ugliness in painting that they have ended up considering it almost indispensable.

"Often when people very involved in modern painting find themselves in front of a high-quality canvas—painted well and with indisputable painterly value—they remain silent without expressing an opinion. They are distrustful because of the fact that they *sincerely like* the painting.

"The continual habit of viewing horrible paintings, which are nevertheless considered masterpieces and sold for extremely high prices, has removed people's faith in their own judgment. The opinion has taken hold in their minds that a truly good modern painting *cannot be enjoyed*, and if you enjoy it, it means that it is not good, even that it is *pompier. Pompierism* is despised by the moderns. And so it often happens that in front of a beautiful painting, today's amateurs maintain a prudent silence. They believe it is better not to compromise themselves, and they don't dare speak of sincerity, atmosphere, emotion, mystery; and even particular words like *arabesque*, which they pronounce with great sureness before a certain kind of modern painting, seem to them in this case dangerous.

"Their greatest fear is to seem stupid and ignorant, speaking well of a painting that, according to modern opinion, is clearly not worth anything, seeing as they feel pleasure looking at it. So it is that lovers and collectors of art today understand painting.

"Now, on the subject of critique, there are those who aren't only uninterested in painting, but also detest it openly and prefer as a consequence not to look at the paintings that are shown to them. Such people have discovered a manner of looking at a painting—from above, from below, from the side, but never head-on. The more well-known a critic is, the greater his virtuosity in writing very obscure and complicated articles about paintings he has scarcely glimpsed. What matters in these articles is only his personality, his intelligence, and not the painting, which for him is only a pretense for showing off.

"Most critics express the most unexpected things in their articles, things that have nothing to do with the paintings they are discussing.

"In general, most of an article about modern painting consists of a series of sentences and words that don't express even a clear idea about a work's painterly value. These are vague remarks, which resemble the delirium caused by fever more than they do a logical and serious analysis of the values of a work of art. These articles often have shorter sections whose significance is sometimes clearer, where, with surprising candor, the critic expresses judgments of this sort: for example, in a painting where the outlines are drawn with fat black or dark-blue brushstrokes at least two fingers thick, instead of simply seeing the coarseness and clumsiness of the execution, the critic perceives the 'force.' It is above all when discussing paintings depicting large characters with hypertrophic arms and legs that the modern Aristarchuses say, *This painting has much force*. Logically, this must signify that the volume of the character depicted determines the force with which a canvas has been painted.

"In other words, a Rubens painting must have much force because he painted very large women. (For this reason, the modernists don't trust themselves on the subject of Rubens and would prefer not to speak on it.) Raphael's paintings would be of medium force because they depict figures of average volume, and the works of Botticelli, who painted very slender and thin women, must be considered absolutely *weak*. We'll add that Michelangelo is always called a *titan* or a *giant*, no doubt because his sculptures and paintings display bodies laden with muscles expressing physical power. They call him *titan* for an external reason and without thinking at all about the force of his talent and the greatness of his artistic personality.

"If the definition of *titan* had a spiritual origin, I don't see why we wouldn't also call Phidias a titan—his talent is no less gigantic and powerful than Michelangelo's. And yet, the words *giant* and *titan* are never employed when speaking of Phidias. By the same token, force is never mentioned in reference to Fragonard or François Boucher, because one believes that force of talent cannot be expressed in a painting of an idyllic countryside or a beautiful nude. We have, alas, an ingénue's freshness in our judgments about art, which seems a bit much, especially as, from the artistic point of view, we are not such novices at all. It is enough to simply walk through the interminable rooms of museums to realize that by now we should have developed a mode of assessment that is more just and better aligned to the truth than what we use today when speaking or writing about art.

"Now, I have already said this, Maestro, but I will repeat it: the only value that exists in certain modern pictures is the *value of revelation* (*when* this phenomenon exists, as it is in fact very rare).

"In ancient painting, on the contrary, value exists in the *inspiration*.

"To avoid any ambiguity, I must make you understand that inspiration in the works of the old masters is not, as it is generally and naively believed, a question of composition, subject, and image, but only and above all a question of *the beauty of the painterly material*, a question of supreme mastery of execution, of plastic power, that is, of the exceptional *qualitative* value of the work.

"I must add that *inspiration* and *revelation* are mysterious phenomena; they are most difficult to define and absolutely cannot be provoked or forced by the artist's will.

"They are phenomena that appear in the mind of the artist without him being able to say with precision from where or how they have arrived.

"Now, Maestro, I will begin to define the difference between inspiration and revelation. Inspiration is a grace that God has granted to a person he has chosen as an instrument for revealing to other people the expressions of the Universal Talent. How can one imagine that without any superior influence a person's talent can create paintings like those of Titian, Rubens, Velázquez or music like that of Chopin, Schubert, Bellini?... From where might this flow of inspiration come if not from the existence of the Universal or Superior Talent, true creator of Art? A great artist is the elect through which the Universal and Divine Talent expresses itself in a form that is ideal but comprehensible to men. And it is from the Divine Talent, which can also be called the Cosmic, that the artist arrives at inspiration.

"Revelation, on the other hand, is another phenomenon, not tied to the Superior Talent and consequently not found in direct relation to art. The revelation expressed in certain works of art is a purely modern phenomenon that is not found in the paintings of the ancient artists, except in a fragmentary manner in the works of Dürer. In some Poussin paintings and perhaps even some by Claude Lorrain, a phenomenon approaches revelation but should instead be defined as the ingenious interpretation of legend.

"The phenomenon of revelation began to be manifest in the nineteenth century in certain works by painters, philosophers, and poets.

"We can define the moment in which a man has a revelation as the instant during which he has been able to glimpse a world outside of those things known to the human spirit. It is a world that human logic cannot conceive of, and it does not exist for mortals—for us, all that effectively exists is that which we recognize, or at most, things whose possible existence we can imagine.

"That metaphysical world, nonexistent for us, or that world completely beyond human knowledge and conception which we, with our brains, don't perceive, is the world that Nietzsche and Hölderlin allowed us to glimpse in some fragments and some poems.

"In painting, in various works by painters of the second half of the last century and of our century, painters like Böcklin, Max Klinger, Previati, Picasso, and Giorgio de Chirico, an image of this mysterious world is traced. It has to do with an inexplicable world that the intelligence can merely feel through intuition but that is impossible to comprehend or describe by means of logic.

"The painting made by a painter following a revelation presents an aspect of the world that is unknown and strange to us. The execution of such a painting might be reduced to an image correctly sketched, as the worth of a piece of this kind doesn't consist in the quality of the painting, but in the spiritual content. I want to repeat once more, Maestro, that comprehending revelation is difficult for a person who is not gifted with exceptional intelligence, and it is precisely this that has allowed *invented* painting to take on this appearance, not only stupid and ridiculous, but also absurd.

"People believe that it is enough to put the most bizarre objects in a painting and add lines and forms provided that they seem odd, in order for the painting to acquire value as something of the spirit. Mediocre painters who witness the success of paintings depicting truly strange worlds that the authors of these paintings have glimpsed do not understand that these paintings, at base, are nothing but the fruit of the artist's revelation. As such, they continue to believe that they can substitute eccentricity and originality for true revelation. Revelation permits us to see a metaphysical world that exists beyond men, while the effort toward eccentricity and originality gives rise to a stupid and absurd world *made by men*.

"From this lack of understanding of supernatural and inexplicable worlds and from the impossibility for mediocre men to conceive of it, pseudospiritual, surrealist, so-called invented painting is born; but it is *invented terribly*.

"These petty and pitiful ideas created by the small fantasies of men who aren't true artists have replaced the metaphysical world for the ignorant, for those who follow the fashions of intellectualism. What a sad result for those artists who have been in contact with a metaphysical world, to see this idiotic and earthly world completely unrelated to metaphysical concerns that the mediocre painters have tirelessly reproduced in innumerable paintings, while the intellectuals, too, have taken complete stupidity for superior intelligence, accepting pseudospiritual painting without being able to comprehend or even guess the existence of the *phenomenon of revelation*.

"Now, Maestro, I will analyze for you some aspects of modern painting.

"Pompierism and modernism are not entirely different in the quality of their respective paintings. These two movements, which believe themselves to be so unrelated to each other, have in common the ugliness of their material, which is not material from a painterly point of view but dried-up oil paint.

"Pompier painters often have some ability, but completely lacking in them is the sense of painterly material on which the quality of an artwork depends. As a result, they have known less well than others how to adapt themselves to modern taste, which is ultimately a reaction to the style of the nineteen hundreds and seeks simplicity and sobriety in order to avoid the ornaments of bad taste. The modern eye has adjusted to this lack of ornament. People today prefer to see straight lines, smooth and uninterrupted surfaces, because instinctively, *they do not trust the artistic capacities of their contemporaries.* This is why art lovers have more or less turned toward modernism, leaving pompier painting to the bourgeoisie, who have greater difficulty detaching themselves from the recent past. Nonetheless, it is for absolutely superficial and not at all artistic reasons that the art lover believes that modern painting is true art but pompier painting is not.

"Among the so-called modern painters, there are artists of talent who are in effect greater artists than the pompier painters. But the artistic import of their pictures comes simply from their talent and not the role of the sketch nor the summary execution of their works.

"Art lovers and critics have not understood where the artistic value of these paintings lies, mistaking their defects for their quality. These people believe that simplicity is a quality of art, and they confuse poverty and coarseness with simplicity. There is no evidence that a good painting must be simple. The most beautiful works of the old masters prove the precise opposite is true.

"Those select painters who became famous because they had talent and not, as was the case with others, as a result of the maneuvers of dealers, realized, guided by their talent, that they could make no more than sketches as they did not possess the secrets of painting. They understood that when you don't have the painterly material that truly allows you to paint—that is, to make good paintings—it is preferable to limit yourself to sketches to preserve, at least for the painted image, a more or less artistic aspect.

"Without talent, the majority of modern painters believed that they could imitate the celebrated modern painters and their qualities, substituting a sketch for a completed work. So it is that one can clearly understand that it is not the sketch that determines the artistic aspect of a picture, but the talent with which it is executed. The exaggerated number of painters found today in every country is due to the fact that comprehension of painting is extremely rare, not only in art lovers but also in those who wish to be painters. Those who make pictures today are generally spurred to do so not because of talent but because they believe that the craft can be lucrative as well as easy and not laborious. We can deduce with certainty from the appearance of most modern pictures that it is not at all necessary to have talent or even the skill of an artisan to make them.

"People's hands have lost skill and their brains have lost creative and artistic intelligence. Modern pictures are not good pictures because good pictures cannot exist without good painterly material. The material with which one makes a picture is not a vague thing; it is a concrete entity whose quality is already evident upon the palette that the painter has prepared for his work.

"Like the majority of modern painters, art lovers don't even ask themselves the true meaning of painterly material, and as a consequence they cannot imagine of what elements this material should consist. But true artists, aware of the necessity of finding the secret of the material substance of paint, without which painting cannot return to perfection, search for such material with the greatest ardor.

"They cannot be aided in this research by their talent or work, since the tradition was interrupted around the middle of the nineteenth century; it is necessary to begin again from the start.

"The great interest awakened by the appearance of invented painting in those who understood the phenomenon diminished little by little because it could not long substitute for the true task of the painter, which is *to make paintings*.

"The door to the metaphysical world opens but rarely, such that great painting, tied to the Universal Talent, is the fruit of artistic inspiration along with seriously human and concrete work.

"One of the principal causes of decadence in the arts, perhaps *the* principal cause, is the industrialization and mechanization of all that lends itself to being industrialized and mechanized. For painting, the industrialization of art materials has been enormously harmful. Machines take intelligence from humans. Human hands no longer have the important task of producing the things the human mind invents. Hands have lost and will further lose their capacities and abilities. Cerebral gymnastics are reduced to ever more minor movements because the brain, no longer needing to direct the hands, rigidifies, falls asleep, or settles down depravedly into those sterile and negative forms of intelligence, rooted in malignancy and indiscretion, that have contributed so much to the success of Freudianism and its derivatives.

"If you think that all human intelligence, which is so superior to the intelligence of animals, has its origin and was able to develop thanks to the constructions of human hands and that, if human hands had taken the shape of dog paws or horse hooves, nothing we have created would exist, then you must admit that mechanization—reducing as it does such important creative tasks—diminishes our cerebral capacities and will diminish them ever more.

"Manual labor—in which a person's hand, supervised and guided by his intelligence, produces continual and concrete creation—is necessary for the continuation and development of our intellect's creative capacities, and this industriousness of our hands is indispensable to the reflourishing of both true intelligence and true painting."

Isabella Far quieted, and Mr. Dudron looked at her with a thoughtful expression. Then he said, "How right you are, madam, and how logical and profound is everything you say; I too have frequently observed this, but was not able to articulate it in such a concrete and philosophical manner as you have done. Philosophers are born as painters are born. Unfortunately, today there are those who declare themselves philosophers who are no more than professors of philosophy. The true philosopher is above all an artist, because philosophy is an art.

"Regarding the current damage to creative possibility and the talents and abilities of men produced by mechanical and scientific progress, I'll add that some days ago I was having more or less the same reflections—though in a confused and abstract manner, it's true, because, as I was saying, I certainly do not have your philosophical talent. Several days ago I was reading in a book by a nineteenth-century author a description of an evening, around 1860, in a grand bourgeois family. Among the company there were no musicians, no singers, no actors, no one who was an artist by profession. Yet the young women, girls, engineers, merchants, lawyers, youngsters who hadn't yet completed their studies—all of them had cultivated an art with love and intelligence: someone accompanied singers on the piano and was joined by the chords of a gentleman playing guitar; a young man and lady danced a Spanish dance perfectly; a lady recited verses; with a confident hand, another gentleman executed a pencil portrait of one of the ladies present; and finally, a gentleman who worked as a lawyer performed sleights of hand with a deck of cards and entertained the gathering by putting his hands in front of a lit candle and projecting their shadows against a white sheet hung on the wall. The author of the book said it was truly impressive to see how, with imperceptible movements of his hands, the dilettante magician achieved on the sheet the silhouette of a wolf in the act of devouring a rabbit. You could see the rabbit, ears forward, disappearing slowly into the throat of the wolf, whose eyes widened with satisfaction and whose stomach inflated gradually as the rabbit was consumed!

"In contrast to this scene, a few days ago I spent the evening with a bourgeois family. There, too, were present young ladies, youngsters, and gentlemen, but no one had the least talent for the smallest thing. There was vague discussion of some fashionable literature, political chatter of the stupidest kind, then they began to gossip and bad-mouth a number of people who were not present, and almost everyone, especially the men, made great efforts to seem intelligent and superior. To break the boredom a bit the hostess turned on the radio, which was playing dance tunes and African American songs, and then she put a record of modern music on the gramophone, which everyone listened to while stifling yawns. While the radio and gramophone played, I rightly thought how these two devices, fruits of scientific and mechanical progress, belonged to that genre of objects that have replaced human talent and ability, and the result was this atmosphere of boredom, irritation, and dissatisfaction that weighed heavily on the entire evening.

"You see therefore, madam, that I perceive all these lacks and blanks of our disgraced epoch; it is just that I don't know how to describe them with that instrument of which you have exclusive possession."

They took leave of each other, as Isabella Far had to return home to work. Mr. Dudron did not want to go back to his own house; everything he had heard troubled him. And so, after having said goodbye to Isabella Far and thanked her again, he headed toward the gate on the southern side of the city to take a walk in the countryside nearby.

As was often the case, while he was walking, Mr. Dudron began to think of the long-ago days of his childhood. He saw himself stretched out in bed in his paternal house, looking toward the bare window, and this reminded him of his yearly summer departure for the countryside, and even of his fear of examinations, the pranks of young girls, and, later, military service. From memory to memory he passed into a different version of things. His happiness, he thought, would have been of a different character, mixed with an undefined dread, mixed even with surprise, like finding fish in a subterranean river, or settling down with his own family as a drawing teacher in a municipal school in the center of that melancholy city he glimpsed once, that city without suburbs, isolated from the rest of the world and situated at the base of a valley encircled with mountains that were high and severe. There, Mr. Dudron would finally have found peace, and he would have been able to lead a tranquil life filled with inner joy. In the mornings he would have risen early and, after having his caffe latte on a windowed veranda overlooking a small stream edged by dark stones covered with moss and ferns where his child, outfitted with a sea-green net, would have fished for trout for lunch, he would have gotten his walking stick and hat, and with the springy step of a man who is satisfied and in good health, he would have gone to school by foot. From ten to noon he would have taught a drawing class, correcting the work of his students, whom he would have advised in the method for making shadows with a pencil, carefully crosshatching parallel lines. He would have ambled for two hours among the casts and lithographs depicting farmers in picturesque costumes in the Roman countryside holding jugs and leaning against ruins, or else among reproductions of so-called expressive portraits of Mary Magdalene, eyes raised to the sky and mouth bitter, or Alexander the Great, head inclined above his shoulders, of Belisarius, of dead-eyed Homer, and still among feet in different positions and of every kind—legionnaires' feet, actors' feet shod in buskins, feet of gods and nymphs wrapped in ribbons, feet of dancers in agile poses full of grace—and hands of warriors clenching the sheaths of their swords, or hands of orators stretched toward invisible crowds in the gesture that accompanies and underscores the word, hands of women in charming poses in the act of raising a veil or in poses full of tenderness, clasping to their breasts the heads of babies with chubby cheeks and ringlets in their hair.

At noon his class would have ended; then Mr. Dudron would have walked to the port to watch the departing ships bursting with men and merchandise, or he might have chatted with the Sirens who precisely at noon each day emerge from the water and, after lifting themselves with difficulty upon the blocks of the dam under construction, stretch out to warm themselves in the sun, or sometimes recline, chin in hand, looking with an infinitely nostalgic air at the city with its smoking factories, its cathedral, the towers of its town hall, the river that runs through the middle of the city—that river all shining under the sun and traversed by bridges that are true works of art. Sadly dreamy, the Sirens listen to the sounds of that life that they will never know.

Mr. Dudron's thoughts drifted toward the most beautiful of those Sirens, drifted ceaselessly. He saw her like one of those figures you see in a dream: she had a gaze like that of a statue, and in a quiet voice, a bit raspy, she spoke to him of her son, her Alfredo, whom she had left behind in that distant, barely civilized city. She wanted him to be a painter because, though he was only eight years old, he had already shown a great predisposition for painting. Having received as a Christmas present a box of watercolors, Alfredo had painted the magnificent head of a roaring tiger on a piece of paper; everyone who had seen the picture agreed that the wild beast's ferocious expression was impressive. Another time Alfredo was in a restaurant having breakfast with an uncle who, as a result of a bad investment, was in miserable straits. When the waiter brought the check, the uncle realized he didn't have sufficient money to pay; Alfredo took a plate, blackened it under the flame of several matches, and then, with his uncle's tiepin, drew in the black surface the magnificent head of an Arabian horse with glowing eyes and quivering nostrils. This drawing was executed with so much talent that when he offered it to the owner of the restaurant as payment for the check, the owner looked surprised and declared that he considered himself generously paid with that small masterpiece.

But Alfredo's career could not be, at least for the moment, the subject of Mr. Dudron's concern; he had seen enough to know from experience that what people say counts only for so much. Mr. Dudron mistrusted child prodigies, although in the case of Alfredo he thought it was a different matter and the youngster was simply gifted.

"And then," thought Mr. Dudron, "it's not nothing that he is the child of a Siren. I myself have heard it said that the children of Sirens have, among other things, the fortune in life of never falling in love with a woman; they are immune from this danger because they are always in love with their mothers. Moreover, Sirens conserve their youth and beauty for a long time, and I heard it once from a merchant marine captain who knew the child of a Siren, a man of sixty well-lived years, whose mother was still very desirable. This captain said it was all due to the salt water—and that's why he made his wife bathe in seawater even in the dead of winter, emptying into their bathtub huge buckets that the servants filled every morning at the dam in order to avoid the danger of typhoid fever, which they would have had to fear had they had the imprudence to fill the buckets at the quay where the sewers flow into the sea."

At this point Mr. Dudron had been beyond the city for some time. He interrupted the course of his memories, fantasies, and dreams and began to observe the countryside surrounding him. He was now walking slowly, smoking his pipe and looking around. At this point the river was very wide and muddy; it flowed slowly and sparkled here and there below the pale rays of a stingy sun. The steep slope of the right bank, which was higher, contrasted with the left bank, whose shore was lapped by the water's gentle frothing. From there stretched vast fields of grain and corn, and here and there large garden plots. Everywhere, irrigation canals, placed knowledgeably, channeled and dispersed abundant water. Near the towns of grayish houses, clumps of trees rose, old apples and even eucalyptus, some of their leaves burned in last summer's heat wave, which had been particularly harsh. On the embankments sat numerous fishermen who followed the smallest movements in the drift of their lines with attention. At each sound of the passing boat horns, ducks, ravens, crows, magpies, and sparrows rose from the tall grass. While in that moment the large road beside the river was deserted, the movement of the boats exiting and reentering the water never diminished. There were torpedo boats with their cannons painted gray, some covered by waterproof canvases with a mosaic of oil stains, there were also customs lifeboats and merchant ships with enormous tonnage, and even svelte, elegant yachts with freshly varnished sides, which passed, pulling dinghies as if they were small toys.

As Mr. Dudron went farther, the hamlets became rarer. On the banks, wood ovens smoked, and their smoke, rising into the air in eddies, mixed with the exhaust from the boats. Evening descended sweetly; the air cooled and the half moon shone in the clear sky. Then, a chain of white dunes—arranged symmetrically with a uniform outline—took shape, shaded in the twilight. Mr. Dudron realized that he was now very far from the city. He felt a bit tired. As he was also thirsty, he thought it would be sensible to rest and drink something before embarking on his return. A small tavern was open at the end of the street, and a few rustic tables surrounded by chairs were positioned in front of the door. To the left of the door was a large window in the middle of which were painted two billiard sticks crowning three balls in the shape of a pyramid.

Mr. Dudron sat down at one of the tables and called out for drink service. Then, as no one answered his call, he got up and approached the door of the tavern. The interior of the locale was very dark, and he could not distinguish anyone though he was probably very visible to those inside because he heard a familiar voice calling him by name. Immediately there appeared in front of him a man with a cordial and intelligent face whom Mr. Dudron grasped warmly by the hand. It was a painter Mr. Dudron had met two years before and befriended, realizing that that painter had very sound and normal ideas about art; that is, he loved beautiful painting, detested the bluffs of those paintings lacking form and substance, those pale and flat paintings known as modern that, under the aegis of pseudosensibility and pseudointelligence, hide the most absolute impotence and ignorance. Mr. Dudron invited his friend to sit at his table. Finally the waiter arrived and they ordered a half liter of that slightly sweet and smoky wine that Mr. Dudron particularly liked and which was a specialty of the region. "Regarding this wine, my dear colleague," said Mr. Dudron, "here, they observe traditions that date back to Roman times. In his verses Catullus speaks of that famous *fumosus phalernus*—a highly esteemed wine in the poet's time, which came from the vineyards cultivated in the *agrum phalernum* region of Naples. Catullus rightly called the wine *fumosus* because it tasted of smoke. Indeed, the Romans were in the habit of putting their wines into great terra-cotta amphoras. In the top part of their houses, below the roof, they kept enough sand so that the amphoras, which came to a point, could be plunged in and remain upright. Then, through a hole opened in the paneling near where the amphoras were placed in the sand, the smoke from the *focus*, the fireplace, passed, and so it was that after some time the wine took on the flavor of smoke. In addition, the Romans often made the wine sweeter when drinking it by adding honey. Probably this wine that we now have in front of us is not very different from that which graced Catullus's table."

Speaking thus, Mr. Dudron refilled his friend's glass and then his own and drank after having been wished in return all the good in the world.

At first, they spoke about various topics, and then they began to talk about painting, which was their favorite subject.

Mr. Dudron's friend was a very serious painter who loved his art and sought continuously to perfect it. He had had it with the majority of modern painters who so disregard form or, more accurately, disregard it perforce because they are incapable of demonstrating it. "Don't you find, dear colleague," he said, turning toward Mr. Dudron, "that painters today don't have any sense of form? It is however form that is most important in painting; without form a picture cannot exist, and the entire evolution of the art is a continual effort to perfect the form. But so it is that the form, justly, is also the most difficult thing to realize on a canvas and, as you well know, it took centuries and centuries to arrive at the perfection and mastery of Titian, Velázquez, or Rubens. Concerning these problems of form, which, in connection to painting, preoccupy me more than any others, I read a very interesting article in an art magazine published in my town. The magazine is called *Talent*. It is very well done—it is a magazine without parti pris and often prints admirable articles by Isabella Far.

The article I read is about this precisely—form in art. I have the magazine in my pocket in case you don't know it; you may read the article if you wish."

"Indeed, my dear friend," answered Mr. Dudron, "I don't know that article but I know the writer Isabella Far very well and consider her a true phenomenon of intelligence and philosophical talent. I see her frequently and spend whole hours at a time listening to her extraordinary discourses about painting and many other things. If you wish to read me this article about form, I would be very happy to listen."

Mr. Dudron's friend got up and went to look for the magazine in the pocket of his coat; when he returned, he took a sip of wine, lit his pipe, and began to read:

"'Form in Art and Nature,' by Isabella Far.

"Form is undeniably the essential expression of the plastic arts. The more a painting or a sculpture is perfected, the more perfectly form is expressed within it. Form confers nobility, beauty, and mystery to a painting or sculpture.

"The expression of form reached its apex during the most evolved and felicitous eras of art. It is during those eras that the genius and talent of painters and sculptors reached their full development. During those golden centuries of human genius the ideal form was realized. The idea, which is in itself an abstract phenomenon, became wholly manifest in a plastic and concrete form. The golden centuries of which I speak are the Renaissance and the era that followed, not at all the era of primitive art when they were simply not able to realize their ideas or conceptions fully.

"In great works of art, form is evident at the same time as it is unreal. One might say that form does not belong to this world so much as melt into the surrounding atmosphere, and this fusion completely frees it from that hardness things have in reality.

"The expression *stark reality* no doubt originates in that hardness of the forms surrounding us.

"To be able to express form as separate from the atmosphere even as it is fused with the atmosphere—and therefore mysterious and unreal—has necessitated a progressive and constant effort of the intelligence, affording artists the mastery necessary for the completion of such a task.

"Not only in art but also in nature, form is the *expression of universal evolution*.

"From infancy humans are drawn instinctively to create forms. Even a little child who holds between his hands material that is shapeless but malleable, like sand, earth, or snow, seeks instinctively to mold it into something that can express a form. It is right that this is so because the universe has always transformed shapeless material (the first stage of creation) into matter that expresses itself by means of form (which would be creation at a more advanced stage). The more perfect and complicated the form, the more creation approaches its highest expression, which is *sublime harmony*.

"Great art, through which the Universal Talent is made manifest to men, is the highest expression of creation because it is at once spiritual and material.

"Art is composed of concrete and abstract elements, and it is as tied to the physical world as it is to the metaphysical world, which is to say that art represents the most complete creation that we know.

"Art is the bridge uniting our world and the beyond, and thoughts equipped for the dangerous journey to another world can cross this bridge in complete tranquility and adventure because the return route is secured by the solid construction of the bridge, which cannot collapse. Indeed, cases of madness are extremely rare among artists, while philosophers and other explorers of the unknown are threatened by the insanity that remains by their side, ready to seize them at every opportunity.

"Form in nature results from transformation produced by universal movement. Such form shows us the mystery of creation more obviously than inert material can—material is the starting point, but form is the goal. In art, which is the product of genius, form manifests the mystery of creation in an even more evident way than in nature.

"In painting, form is purely ideal, which is to say, immaterial. In sculpture, on the other hand, concrete form made by a material exists as volume; so in sculpture, mystery is only evident in the execution and in the brilliance of conception.

"In painting, form is much more difficult to realize. While in sculpture one works with a malleable material like clay or wax or with a material that has concrete volume like a block of marble, in painting form is not realized through material with volume although formless in itself, but through a metaphysical material with the help of a physical material which is virtually nonexistent as volume. The actual volume of this material has no direct relationship with the volume of the represented form.

"In painting, volume is made by metaphysical material, which creates, in the fullest sense, material that is physical but not malleable, nonexistent as volume but regardless capable of expressing any volume or whatever form.

"The very origin of painting can be found in the particularity of human thought. Human thought is not expressed, as it is falsely believed, by means of words. The classic question posed to people who speak more than one language fluently—'In which language do you think?'—is curious in this regard. The question doesn't make sense because we don't think in any languages at all. Instead, thoughts are a series of images or figurations that pass with extraordinary rapidity through the human brain. Images or visions in which form is the dominant element are precise when they pertain to a perfectly defined and individuated object, and they are imprecise if the object is more or less a concept, that is to say, when the object has a particular form but without the specific details that characterize it. Here is an example to further clarify: a person has a house; thinking of the house, she sees in her spirit all the detail that distinguishes it. In this case the image that presents itself to the spirit is precise. When, on the other hand, for whatever reason, a person is obliged to look for a house, she thinks of a house that is still unknown and her brain reflects the image of the concept she has of houses in general. This is an imprecise image that nevertheless expresses the form of a house but without the specifics that define it.

"Thoughts and visions undeniably have their colors, but their principal force *resides in the expression of their form.*

"The abstract form expressed in these image-thoughts, the form thought produces without the help of material with a concrete volume, has led humans to draw and paint.

"The thesis that thought is an image or vision is confirmed in ancient Egyptian writings by the very fact that the first writings were drawings of the things described. It is important to add that these drawings presented the form and not the color of the objects they were meant to represent.

"Humans have sought to express their thoughts without recourse to an intermediary—in this case, the word. They have turned directly to the image, which is the expression of form realized by thought, without the help of concrete and malleable material.

"It is important to add that form, being the base of thought, represents at the same time the foundation upon which all of our intelligence rests.

"Form reflected by our brains gave us the possibility of thinking. Immaterial form has allowed our thoughts to multiply, to move further and further away from reality, permitting us to enter thus into abstraction. Philosophy, music, science—everything is born from form. All of these creations of our spirit have as their origin form produced by nature, then and above all, immaterial form, namely, the ideal.

"This immaterial or ideal form is born from direct form or, in other words, from form that exists in nature.

"As the light of the sun is caught and reflected by the moon, so too direct form is registered by the human brain, which has projected it into the world. This has initiated the gradual development of human intelligence.

"When one understands the importance of form—when one understands the significance of form as the result of progressive, necessary, and inevitable evolution—one comes to the conclusion that art that does not express a perfect form (as Greek art does) or that, at least, doesn't express form in the most perfect manner possible (as one can observe later in the great eras of artistic production), a plastic art in which form has disappeared, as we see today, is a negative phenomenon that proves that genius, and even good sense, have fallen into decadence. In contemporary art, in painting as well as sculpture, form is almost always nonexistent.

"In modern sculpture, hardness and rigidity have taken the place of plasticity and artistic volume. Concrete form—which past masters rendered mysteriously elusive through their talent—that form that seemed unreal even when representing forms that exist in reality, that magic form that no longer has a place in our time, has disappeared like the past. And when I look at sculpture made today, it seems I am butting my eyes against a hardness much greater than the hardness forms have in reality.

"In modern painting, form—or, rather, those blots that should represent it—gives the impression of something monstrous, irritating, and aplastic. In modern works, form is concave instead of convex. A form that is essentially concave is the negation of form or the annulment of form, which, in this case, is substituted by a void.

"The nonexistence of form in modern painting is a consequence of the nonexistence of volume; yet things are manifest to us first through their volume and only then through their color.

"The explanations people have attempted regarding the lack of form in modern painting don't change this fact in the slightest. I would like to cut all this chatter short by affirming that form in painting is form that the artist's talent has grasped *through intuition*. This form is transformed and transmitted to us through the genius of the painter without the artist's human reason, which remains outside of his genius and does not contribute to the creation of that form.

"This is because a true work of art must not compel the viewer or creator toward reason, criticism, surprise, or divagation, but must elicit only satisfaction and nothing more than satisfaction—that is, a state in which reason no longer exists.

"The avalanche of words, explanations, suppositions, irritation, senseless discussions, etc., generated by modern art demonstrates that *modern art does not elicit satisfaction*. A satisfied person is silent, this is why today the lovers, producers, and all those who support modern art talk and talk without pause. . . ."

Having completed his reading of Isabella Far's article on form, Mr. Dudron's friend was quiet. Mr. Dudron, too, remained in silence. He relit his pipe, got up, and went to the counter to pay for the bottle of wine. Then he returned to his friend and suggested they leave and walk a stretch of road together.

"With pleasure, dear colleague," answered his friend. "I will happily accompany you for a bit. It is a magnificent evening—tranquil and warm. After having read this excellent article on form, I would very much like to recount something else that does not relate directly to painting but all the same merits attention from a man such as you, who has the eminently concrete spirit of a superior artisan joined with the profound soul of a poet and metaphysician. No doubt you know, my dear friend, that in the neighborhood or part of the city where I live there is a rise, a sort of hill bordered on one side by rocks—it looks like a cliff of Gothic apostle profiles jutting out over the city's white expanse of houses—and on the other side by a gentle slope that descends from the summit to the plain. On that hill you can see the white contours of temples, sanctuaries, and other ancient monuments; they are, rather, the outline of all that is left of these monuments because they are all more or less in ruins and their remains lie on the ground beside the parts still standing. In the evening when the air is clear and the moon bathes the sleeping acropolis with its sweet light, the spectacle is so suggestive, so charming, that one has the feeling another happiness exists up there, of a profundity barely expressible, that there reigns a serenity only the great poets and thinkers, strolling slowly among the trees of paradise, seem capable of knowing. In short, one has the impression of an atmosphere so different from all that surrounds us that more than once I have been tempted to spend the whole night there, a night lit by a full moon, alone, amid the ruins, with the city immersed in its nocturnal repose at my feet and above my head, the vast vault of the eternal sky.

"I have visited that acropolis many times, and I have passed many unforgettable hours losing myself in fantasies and meditations of every kind in front of those sublime relics of a glorious past. But this has always taken place during the day, in the midst of crowds of tourists and visitors, under the irritating glare of the guards—while what I desired, the fantasy I nurtured, was to spend the whole night there, a beautiful moonlit night, completely alone. This is however not an easy thing to do because after sunset the entrance gates are closed like the doors of a museum.

"Indeed, that acropolis is now treated precisely like a museum and not a place of poetry and meditation that everyone may enter freely, like a church.

"In my father's day, access to the acropolis was unrestricted both day and night. Today, however, this has changed. You must pay an entrance fee during the day, and during the night, no matter how strong your desire to enter might be, there is nothing to be done—you must give it up.

"They say this is because of the pairs of lovers who would visit during the night and in the midst of those ancient ruins surrender themselves to amusements that were not at all chaste. This is no doubt true, but they could have just posted some severe watchmen assigned to night surveillance or threatened a steep fine or even a few months in prison for those violating the rules or offending decency with their behavior.

"Finally, last summer, no longer able to resist, I began to think seriously about how I might be able to hide myself in the acropolis in the evening before closing and spend the night.

"I recalled having so often observed those insects called centipedes, which horrify me because they make me think of fleeing filth. When one of these insects travels along a wall or some other surface and encounters a mark that seems to have a tint or tone similar to its own, it stops and remains still because it feels that it will be less visible, and in this way it hopes to escape the danger that threatens it. Quail do the same thing. My father, who was a great hunter and continued to hunt even when he was very old, would tell me of that migratory bird whose head, as you too have so frequently mentioned to me, is so disquieting—my father told me that when this bird lands on terrain whose color resembles that of its feathers, it doesn't move; it avoids making the least movement even when a hunter nears, and sometimes the hunter will pass by the quail without seeing it.

"Thinking precisely of those curious instincts that animals and even insects possess, I got the idea to dress in white in order to be less visible amid the whiteness of the ruins. I acquired, therefore, a suit of white fabric, white shoes with rubber soles, a white beret. I put white woven gloves and a box full of talc and white rice powder in my pocket. I shaved with care, and on the afternoon of a day when I knew there would be a full moon, I paid my entrance ticket and, with the most natural demeanor in the world, entered the acropolis.

"I began to stroll among the temples and sanctuaries. I looked at the countryside that stretched across the distance to the sea, which shone on the horizon. I pretended to be interested in the movements of the visitors who, books in hand, would look at the monuments and then consult their books and then look once more at the monuments, while on their faces one could clearly see that the activity provided them with relatively little pleasure. It is strange—I have often asked myself why so many adults who are perfectly free in their actions and can spend their days at their leisure so frequently impose upon themselves the effort of spending entire days going around museums, tiring themselves out and getting stiff necks from the strain of holding their heads up to look at frescoes or paintings on the ceiling. And I ask myself, too, how it is that other adults (often the very same ones), who are perfectly free and masters of their own activities, feel compelled to go to concerts and remain seated for hours, immobile but visibly exhausted, to listen to interminable symphonies that can last more than an hour.

"On this subject I remember that when I was a youth my mother would bring me on trips and when we visited a city with an important museum, we would go to the museum and, after looking at paintings that didn't really interest me, I would return to the hotel completely exhausted, as if I were in the grip of an attack of influenza. But as I was then very young I had no choice because I had to obey my mother. If I had been free in my actions, if I could have done what I wanted, you can be certain, dear friend, I would not have tired myself out like that; I would instead have spent the day in a bakery eating desserts with whipped cream and chocolate ice cream.

"As I was saying, there are many adults, free to do as they please, who understand painting maybe even less than I understood it when I visited museums with my mother. As a result, these people don't feel any pleasure when they look at a painting, no matter how beautiful and perfect it may be, and they impose unpleasant things upon themselves with discipline worthy of a better cause.

"But let's get back to my visit to the acropolis. There I was, strolling through the ruins, waiting anxiously for time to pass and the closing hour to come. Time passed, and the sun descended on the horizon. The sounds of the city reached me; I listened to the intense buzzing of that immense beehive made of so many white cubes lined up in a row. But even that drone receded little by little as soon as I heard the nasal, distant voice of a guard shouting, 'Closing time!'

"The fateful moment had arrived. With a distracted air I pretended to head toward the exit and hid behind a pile of ruins. I put on my white gloves and powdered my neck and face generously. Then, in order to be the least visible, I crouched between the stones and waited.

"Toward the east, behind the purple line of the mountains, the moon had appeared. A full moon: magnificent, royal, complete. It rose slowly, still wrapped in the vapors of the day's heat. The sky became darker. I realized that the last visitor had left. Above my head bats appeared, moving through the twilight like intoxicated birds. From far away came the barking of dogs and the sound of a train that was traveling somewhere to the north. I decided not to move until night had descended completely. This was very prudent because seconds later I heard the footsteps of a guard coming slowly toward the place where I was hidden. A shiver traveled down my spine. Two steps away from me the guard stopped; he didn't remotely suspect my presence. I itched terribly all over my body. I looked at the guard and consoled myself with the thought that I wasn't a jackrabbit and he wasn't a hunting dog. I said to myself, 'In any case, he can't detect my smell.' Holding my breath and trying to avoid the slightest movement, I regarded him. He twirled his mustache, gazing into the distance. Then he coughed, spit on the ground, and, removing a pipe from the pocket of his overcoat, filled it with tobacco. I thought of the hunter near the quail he didn't see. The seconds seemed like hours. The guard lit his pipe, spit once more on the ground, and then, slowly, his hands clasped behind his back, walked toward the exit. I began to breathe more freely. But I decided not to make any movements or extend my legs, which were making me suffer cruelly, until I heard the sound of the key locking the gate. Finally I understood that I was alone. Night had come. There at the horizon where the sun had set, a pallid luminosity persisted. On the opposite side, no longer covered by the summer evening's mists, the moon rose in the sky. Its sweet glow, its sweet and solemn glow touched in that moment the columns and ruins and lengthened their shadows upon the ground. The silence became more profound. Suddenly, I heard a strange sound as though above my head an enormous velarium had been pulled back.

"The superhuman masks of the ancients appeared like gigantic models hung against the backdrop of the sky, which seemed low, very low. It felt as though the sky had neared the earth in an unsettling way. I had the impression that rising up onto the tips of my toes or, at most, climbing onto one of the column fragments scattered on the ground, I would have been able to touch it with my fingers. The divine masks were smiling. An indescribable *faith* pervaded everything, and in the ineffable sweetness of that great night I felt that *evil had vanished*. Debts had been paid, punishment abolished, in bulk bad dreams had been buried far away in the burning sands of the godforsaken deserts. Everything that I had loved in my life, everything that had supported me to that point, was with me.

"I wanted to look down and find the city lights because all that beauty and happiness was starting truly to unsettle me, and the value and usefulness of the bad and of daily troubles appeared to me in all of their significance.

"I wanted to look down, but I couldn't see anything.... A sweet sound had risen from the valley, and on that new sea, the acropolis, its moorings broken, sailed as though carried by the wind..."

Mr. Dudron's friend fell silent. Mr. Dudron didn't say anything either, and the two men walked side by side through the night.

Finally they reached the city gates. As both of them were tired from walking for so long, Mr. Dudron invited his colleague and friend up to his rooms to rest a bit and have something to drink.

When they were in his studio, Mr. Dudron invited his friend to settle comfortably into an armchair and, in order to relax more fully, stretch his legs out on a stool. Then Mr. Dudron got a bottle of old wine and two glasses, and while he eased into another chair, poured the wine, and lit his pipe, he began like this: "What you just told me, my dear friend, about your adventure at the acropolis is very beautiful and very profound.

It moved me, and I am truly happy to think that I have friends capable of such rare feelings, such solitary sensations. I too have often dreamed and journeyed in my fantasies along these little-traveled roads where intellectual adventure carries you so far that you risk losing yourself in insanity. That is what happened to Nietzsche.

"We who are artists, and especially us painters, need something more, especially now, as painting struggles in decadence that has no parallel in any moment in the history of art. The most distressing thing is that today there are so many people who in bad faith deny this decadence because it is in their interest to deny it. These people construct theories to seduce the rest. Unluckily for them, the theories stink of opportunism from ten kilometers away. You find these days a kind of bourgeoisification and cowardice that consists in cautiously taking refuge under the protection of modernism and stretching out comfortably beneath the covers of that which is called the artistic avant-garde. These theories, unfortunately for those who espouse them, have a defect—a great defect: they bring to mind the famous fable of 'The Fox and the Grapes.' One senses anxiety in these theories, all the discontent tormenting their authors, and one feels, too, their envy of those who are *capable of reaching the grapes*.

"It is late, my dear friend, I suggest you sleep here and take the train home tomorrow morning. Before we abandon ourselves to the mild arms of Morpheus, I would like to read you something written recently by Isabella Far, that Egerian nymph of us true painters—those of us who work and struggle so that painting can be reborn and art returned to its sanctuary.

The struggle, adventure, and future we see today are because of us; we are the ones who feel the need to fight. While the others out there, those cowards with Frisian hats, sansculottes in house dresses, get all excited, grimacing and twisting their jaundice-tinted faces."

Mr. Dudron got up and walked toward his bookshelf to find the volume of Isabella Far's writings. When he found it, he returned to his friend, opened the book and began reading: "*Portraits and Still Lifes*, essays on critical philosophy by Isabella Far.

"During the golden century of painting, a painting was a work of art. Painters painted paintings with high artistic value, pictures of superior quality, creations that were art.

"In those happy times, lovers of painting were people gifted with a very developed artistic sense, thanks to tradition handed down by their ancestors, and they also had the delicacy and refinedness that originates from true culture.

"Artists and art lovers found themselves on the same intellectual plane; they had the same clarity and superiority of spirit. There was true contact between creators and viewers of art because they were tightly bound by shared comprehension and love for that astonishing and magnificent phenomenon.

"Today, painting is no longer a great art. The painting of our era is decoration and image merchandise, and that which is called modern painting is above all a frenetic search for originality and false aestheticism.

"The real reason for painters' departure from true art, that departure we see among modern artists, resides in the plastic impossibility of superior artistic creation. Creative impotence has obligated modern artists to seek out loopholes and the ersatz. The result is the monotony and profound boredom that emanate from these innumerable paintings, always equal in substance, always of the same inferior quality, in which one finds only very rarely the smallest spark of talent.

"The modern art lover completely deserves the artistic level of our era. He is, if this is possible, even farther from art than today's painters. The modern art lover doesn't even expect a painting to be above all a work of art. He believes that a painting is an image and that its worth depends on the subject it represents. And so, today's art lover has docilely accepted sad landscapes full of mud, nonexistent still lifes with empty figures lacking form. Lovers of modern art content themselves with all these unattractive images for the simple reason that an entire literature accompanies and sustains these pictorial representations which, saying nothing in themselves, have been explained with terms like *spirituality*, *purity*, *sincerity*, and an infinite number of other words that, uttered in reference to a painting, mean absolutely nothing.

"Once and for all we seek to explain to those interested in art that a painting cannot be sincere or pure or spiritual, it can only be well or badly executed, it can have or not have artistic worth. It is simply the quality of a painting that determines whether a painting is a work of art or an ordinary object.

"In this essay I will discuss portraits.

"The portraits painted for the last three-quarters of a century can be divided into two categories: in the first are academic or society portraits and in the second are the portraits we call avant-garde or modern. The academic or society portraits, which are painted by authorized painters or portrait artists tied to the elegant life, are naturally more numerous than the *modern* portraits, and that is because the so-called *modern* portraits can't even satisfy a public so artistically unprepared as today's public. With *unprepared* I refer as much to the bourgeoisie as to the *snobs*.

"Ultimately people want to see themselves represented in a more or less normal way.

"There have been only very few *intellectuals* who have decided to sacrifice their earthly forms on the altar of modernism. From this heroic sacrifice all those flat and lifeless, but thankfully not numerous, intellectual interpretations were born: these are *modern* or avant-garde portraits.

"The academic and society portraits contain less of what today is called *spirituality*, but in exchange they are much more representational. They are less aestheticized but much better drawn. Their defect is that they are not works of art because they are completely lacking in artistic interest and painterly beauty. The principal reason for the antiartistic character of the academic and society portraits resides in the inferior quality of the material with which they have been painted; this material does not allow for the delicacy of modeling, the luminosity of color, the preciousness of fabric, the transparency of shadow—in sum, everything that makes up the mysterious allure of portraits by the great masters like Rubens, Velázquez, Rembrandt, Tintoretto. The difference between an academic or society portrait of our era and a beautiful ancient portrait depends therefore on the bad quality of the material.

"One cannot insist enough on this question of the *quality of the material.* To render the difference between a good and bad painting more evident to the reader, I'll add that the difference between the material in a beautiful ancient painting and the material on a modern canvas is equal to the difference between a precious stone and a pebble.

"The academic and society painters of the end of the last century and the beginning of our own, painters like Bonnat, Carolus-Duran, Zuloaga, Boldini, and others, surely had some ability, some craft, but the paintings they left are not good paintings precisely because of the bad quality of their materials. They will not endure the test of time, time which makes the best selection between true and false values. Who was it who first said that *time puts everything into its proper place*? Time, great consoler and counselor of humans, who are incapable of living or understanding without its help.

"Since the bourgeoisie became the principal purchasers of paintings, painting has degenerated into decoration, a commerce in images, and portraits have become representations without artistic value of the people who have their portraits done.

"Portraiture finds itself in a delicate situation in contemporary painting for the following reason: A portrait is a very difficult subject to paint and in the execution of a portrait, that which succeeds and that which fails is, even for the layman, more evident, more verifiable than it would be with another subject.

"That is why, as I have already illustrated, the majority of people commissioning a portrait prefer the faithfulness of resemblance to modernist and intellectual interpretations.

"By nature, humans are too attached to their physical appearance to sacrifice it in favor of intellectualism and its fashions. Ultimately, even for the most mystical and fervent apostles of modernism, it is much less pleasurable and often even very unpleasant when their theories are applied to a portrait of their own persons. This is why the majority of those who desire their own portraits have turned to academic or society painters and their realistic portraits instead of *modern* and avant-garde painters who would not be able to provide anything but aestheticized interpretations.

"Naturally this preference has greatly irritated the pure intellectuals who, disgusted as a result of a similar lack of comprehension, have treated those realistic but banal portraits with the most profound contempt.

"In their discourses on art, intellectual posers—though firmly set on never commissioning their own portraits—insist upon their implacable conviction that likeness in a portrait is useless, that it is an out-of-date prejudice and only ignorant and stupid people demand it.

"Modern painters are in full agreement about this theory, which for them is very convenient, while the academic and society painters say, and rightly, that this contempt for likeness is due to modern painters' incapacity to achieve it.

"What the *moderns* say—that a portrait must be a spiritual interpretation of the person represented—is simply an excuse that serves to avoid the difficulty involved in realistic portraiture.

"Naturally, I do not accept the idea that spirituality in painting is an idea of the *moderns*.

"In great painting spirituality always exists as a phenomenon inseparable from art. It is a phenomenon that takes multiple forms, as evidenced by the variety and complexity of the same phenomena of the spirit.

"The moderns' so-called intention of breaking away from reality, substituting for it something else, is an effort as absurd as it is useless. Reality cannot exist in painting because in general it does not exist on earth. The universe is solely *a representation of us*. The uniformity with which this representation, or vision, is reflected in men's brains depends merely on the uniformity of the intellectual capacities of men in general, of those who form the bulk of humanity. As a result it is natural that an artist of talent, a person who breaks from the masses, must replace conventional vision or comprehension of the visible world, the common vision of things, with a vision peculiar to him alone, a more perfect vision created by his exceptional possibilities. And with these new and different visions, with the more profound comprehension that great artists have for the things around us, and with these exceptional visions and representations that influence or transform little by little the representations and visions of common humanity, civilization was created over centuries.

"The greater part of humanity is made up of average people who, from parent to child, transmit conventional representations of the world. This communally accepted and conventional comprehension of the phenomena of the universe is modified and transformed gradually thanks to the people of genius who show us other, still unknown aspects of ideas and things. The likeness of a portrait depends on the drawing's exactness and precision, and I am absolutely convinced that the portraits made by the old masters, in addition to being masterpieces (which is to say the highest expression of spirituality), were *perfectly like* the people who posed.

"If a portrait is well drawn, it must be the exact image of the person who sat as a model, and at the same time the portrait *must be a work of art*, which is to say must have a high painterly quality as, in general, all good paintings have.

"A portrait demands great knowledge and mastery of drawing. The slightest error in drawing a portrait changes the expression, changes even the features of a face. Painting a portrait is difficult work that demands matter and materials infinitely superior to the canvases prepared by the kilometer and colors in tubes that are found in shops today. Painting a face is difficult and complicated work that requires precisely those painterly means the old masters had, which afforded artists that first-rate execution of which today even the memory is lost. It is for this reason that so many modern painters dedicate themselves with ardor to still lifes and landscapes, but not still lifes à la Jordaens or Chardin, or landscapes in the manner of Poussin or Rubens.

"Fate has made it so that in the moment in which the bourgeoisie have become the prime consumers of painting, replacing aristocrats and other eminent persons, artists of great talent have become extremely rare among painters. Geniuses have not wished to be born in this era of transition with a new public of unprepared art amateurs.

"Those who have emerged from these social changes must be instinctively drawn toward the material inventions of the human spirit, and, indeed, since the middle of the last century, humans have concerned and applied themselves to their advantage to industrial and mechanical progress and not to the progress of culture. The abrupt disappearance of the artistic sense became virtually universal and extended even into the spheres of eminent and high-ranking people, those characters who, by means of atavistic tradition or their exceptional positions should, more than others, have been able to maintain and conserve their love and comprehension of art.

"Jacques-Louis David was the last great painter to make portraits of illustrious persons. After him society portraiture lost the position it had held in art across the centuries. Ingres did not paint portraits of high-ranking people because of the lack of understanding those personages showed for his work. Delacroix and Courbet considered Napoleon III and his circle incapable of comprehending their paintings. Indeed, as evidence of the period confirms, Napoleon III did not like the paintings of these two great artists. As such society portraits were more frequently commissioned from academic painters because high-ranking people—heads of state, kings, princes, and popes—desired mechanically made portraits and did not have any interest in or love for painting.

"Society portraiture should reassume the position of artistic importance it held in the past and to which it has a right. The banal images to which the portraits of eminent persons have been reduced in our era must not cause people to forget that those who were once the greats of this world were models for artistic genius, and that they spurred the creation of works of inestimable artistic value."

Mr. Dudron paused his reading for a moment while his friend made large gestures of approval and satisfaction. Then his friend said, "How right this all is, my dear Dudron! What amazes me is that even those today who write so many pages on painting, ancient and modern, are not capable of writing something so clear, so logical. When I read and listen to what Isabella Far says about painting and other problems of art and human thought, I feel like I am listening to a poem: a superior lyricism springs from those pages where nothing is left to chance, where everything has surprising clarity and springs from the impulse of a harmonious logic."

"Yes, my friend," answered Mr. Dudron, "I am in absolute agreement; this essay on portraits is a true masterpiece. But before we go to sleep I want to read you another piece on still lifes that is even better. Listen, I'll begin…

" 'Nature Morte.'

"In English and German, the *natura morta* has a different name, which is much more beautiful and correct: *still life* and *Stillleben*—silent life. Indeed, it suggests painting that represents the silent life of objects, a calm life without noise and without movement, existence expressed with volume, form, and plasticity.

"In reality, objects, fruits, leaves, etc., are immobile but can be moved by a human hand or by the wind. Still lifes represent things that are not alive, from the point of view of sound and movement, but that are tied to the life of humans, animals, and plants. These objects are placed on the earth, this earth that with intensity breathes life full of sound and movement.

"On our planet, everything is surrounded by air. Without air everything would be dead. The air envelops our earth and penetrates soft things, silk and velvet fabrics, down feathers, and very ripe fruits.

"When one observes these objects that put up such little resistance to the air, these tender things, pleasurable to touch, one might say that the air girdles them more tightly than it does other objects and merges with them. This close penetration of air that characterizes the reality of tender things must be visible in a painting. Firm bodies with strong surfaces and prominent outlines give the impression of repelling the air, which seems to withdraw and move away from their impenetrable forms and surfaces. The layer of air seems sliced, as though pushed back by the rigid outlines, and it no longer offers our gazes the caressing rest that its soothing presence provides.

"One must be able to paint this play of air that defines and specifies the substance of objects and demonstrates their hardness or tenderness. The substance of a thing matters more than its color. Substance determines form while plasticity is intensified by the layer of enveloping air. Air allows us to intuit and see with our minds aspects of things that are invisible to us. Air allows things to emerge, sweetens their outlines and at the same time intensifies their form. Air is everywhere and *it must also be painted on the canvas*.

"Painting air is very difficult. Painting air means giving a particular plasticity, a particular volume, a particular formal force to things, so that between one object and another you can feel how the air circulates and the objects appear as though suspended, immobile, but *alive* in that air that shifts and moves while the objects seem stopped and immobilized by the effect of some magic.

"In a painting everything depends on the material with which it is painted. The plasticity of forms is as determined by the physical material as by the metaphysical materials peculiar to that painting. The physical material is the tangible body of painting and the metaphysical material is the talent that knew to create that body.

"Beautiful material deployed wisely allows us to see, or better, to feel the air and the effects of its play. When a talented painter paints a still life, he truly paints the *silent life* of those things created by nature or made by humans. Nature and reality have neither aesthetic problems nor artistic preoccupations. It is the artist's duty to give beauty to the things he sees and interprets. A pitcher can be very modest and insignificant, so much so that you don't even notice when you find it on a farmer's table, but in a beautiful painting it can become an object full of nobility and allure.

"The term *natura morta* entered into usage during the last century. This compound word was a real prophecy and has found its full realization in the painting of our age. Modern paintings representing fruits and objects without form or volume are truly pictures of *nature morte* given that the things represented therein—flat, unreal, and without air—are *truly dead*.

"In front of a beautiful still life simple people without intellectual pretensions frequently exclaim, 'Those apples and those oranges seem so real, you might touch them! Look at that cluster of grapes, they make me want to pick them up and eat them!' These enthusiastic and innocent exclamations, these words full of sincerity, are a warning to those intellectuals who are not yet submerged in the mud of snobbism, to those intellectuals in whom snobbism might not only atrophy but also abolish completely every human feeling of joy and pleasure. And I'd say it doesn't matter at all if these simple, sincere, and enthusiastic people can utter the same words in front of a painting of questionable artistic worth; this has no importance because what counts is the sincere joy a person feels in front of a painting. Nevertheless, the joy aroused in the soul of a simple person by a true work of art is stronger and more profound than that which is produced by an image that merely pleases. The joy experienced before a painting engenders the hope that there will come a day when this joy will be justified by the beauty of painting newly reborn on the earth.

"Let us change the name of *natura morta*, offered in a moment of prophetic inspiration to paintings representing things and objects. Let us call these paintings *Silent Lives*. Perhaps this new name can help to abolish the sinister prophecy that has now fully come to be...."

Mr. Dudron closed the book. "Let's go to sleep," he said to his colleague. "I offer you my bed; I will lie down on the couch in my studio. We have talked of so many things, so many things people today are in the habit of going back and forth about."

Mr. Dudron wished his friend good night; then he undressed, lay down, and, tired after a day so full of great and beautiful intellectual adventures, did not delay in falling asleep.

Now, gracious Readers, the author of these pages will also go to sleep. He too is tired, and it is late, almost one in the morning. He will lie down and sleep until noon at least; he has always needed a lot of sleep, and this after all is totally normal because, as Arthur Schopenhauer used to say, a long sleep is indispensable to persons of genius.

FIN.

NOTES ON THE EARLY HISTORY OF THE NOVEL

1929 Giorgio de Chirico's novel *Hebdomeros* is published in Paris by Éditions du Carrefour.

1931 Early traces of *Mr. Dudron* are found in a letter de Chirico wrote to his mother on August 31, 1931. In the letter, he asks her to recover two notebooks from a room in Paris where he had previously worked: "They were on that shelf with the dust-colored glass cups. One notebook has a novel I started, the other some poems: if you could track them down, possibly in the cellar, and send them to me I would be very glad." In a 1932 letter, he wrote to his mother that he had received what he had requested.

1934 "Une nuit sur l'Acropole," a passage from the manuscript (at that point under the working title *Monsieur Dusdron*), is published in *Le voyage en Grèce: cahiers périodiques de tourisme* (Paris: Société Neptos).

1936 De Chirico gives a manuscript with corrections (the title already changed from *Dusdron* to *Dudron*) to Julien Levy on the occasion of his exhibit at Levy's gallery in New York. In his *Memoir of an Art Gallery* (1977), Levy mentions and quotes from the manuscript.

1937 While in New York, de Chirico writes a new chapter of the novel on Barbizon-Plaza Hotel stationery.

1938 *Deux fragments inédits* appears as part of the series Un Divertissement (Paris: Henri Parisot).

1940 In April, de Chirico publishes the story "Una gita a Lecco" in the magazine *Aria d'Italia*; this excerpt will become the opening of the novel.

In May, "Il Signor Dudron (dal romanzo da pubblicare)" is published in *Prospettive* 5.

1941 "Avventura del Signor Dudron" is published in *Corriere Padano*.

1942 "Gedanken des Herrn Dudron"—the German translation of the episodes published in *Prospettive* in 1940—is published in *Italien*.

1945 French versions of "Una gita a Lecco" and other passages from the novel are published as *Une aventure de M. Dudron* as part of Henri Parisot's L'Age d'or series (Paris: Fontaine).

Commedia dell'arte Moderna—the first section attributed to de Chirico and the second to Isabella Far—collects essays on painting written from 1918 to 1945 by de Chirico. Among these essays, "Form in Art and Nature," "Portraits," and "Still Lifes" also appear in *Mr. Dudron*, attributed to Isabella Far.

Details for this timeline were provided by the Fondazione Giorgio e Isa de Chirico.

NOTES AND ACKNOWLEDGMENTS

The passages in the text from J. F. L. Mérimée's *The Art of Painting in Oil and in Fresco: Being a History of the Various Processes and Materials Employed, from Its Discovery, by Hubert and John* [*sic*] *van Eyck, to the Present Time* are quoted directly from W. B. Sarsfield Taylor's translation (London: Whittaker & Co., 1839), accessed through HathiTrust.

The three essays attributed to Isabella Far in the text—"Form in Art and Nature," "Portraits," and "Still Lifes"—were published in *Commedia dell'arte moderna*, attributed to Isabella Far (Rome: Traguardi, 1945). "Form in Art and Nature" appeared prior to that, attributed to de Chirico, in *L'Illustrazione Italiana* (March 1943). In this volume, all three essays appear in my own translation.

* * *

I am grateful to the Fondazione Giorgio e Isa de Chirico for their permission to translate and publish this novel.

This work was supported by fellowships from the National Endowment for the Arts and the 2022 ViceVersa Italian-English translation workshop organized by Richard Dixon, Marina Pugliano, and Anna Rusconi and funded by Translation House Looren. This translation owes a dose of magic to the eyes, minds, and intense attention of the translation family I found at Villa Garbald: Clarissa Botsford, Richard Dixon, Giovanna Granato, Matt Holden, Lachlan Hughes, Anna Mioni, Alta Price,

Anna Rusconi, Laura Scarmoncin, Giovanna Scocchera, and Stefania Zampiga.

Huge thanks to all those who have read, discussed, and wrestled with this novel alongside me, especially: Julia Heim, Jennifer Kronovet, Peter Pihos, and Sally Scopa. Brett Fletcher Lauer launched me on this de Chirico journey, and I am forever grateful. Katherine Robinson's profound de Chirico knowledge, keen close reading, and warm conversation have been indispensable. Thanks to my students and colleagues for their support along the way. And thanks, especially, to my daughters, who would cure even grumpy Mr. Dudron of his hatred of children.

Thanks to everyone at A Public Space, particularly Anne McPeak for her thoughtful copyediting. Finally, my deepest gratitude goes to Brigid Hughes—for believing in this project and for moving mountains to make it a book.